7-99

A *Witness*
to *Life*

By Terence M. Green from Tom Doherty Associates

Shadow of Ashland
Blue Limbo
A Witness to Life

A *Witness* to *Life*

Terence M. Green

A TOM DOHERTY ASSOCIATES BOOK
NEW YORK

This is a work of fiction. All the characters and events portrayed in this novel are either fictitious or are used fictitiously.

A WITNESS TO LIFE

Excerpts from *The Sign of Jonas* by Thomas Merton, copyright 1953 by the Abbey of Our Lady of Gethsemani and renewed 1981 by the Trustees of the Merton Legacy Trust, reprinted by the permission of Harcourt Brace & Company. Excerpt from *The Ascent to Truth* by Thomas Merton, copyright 1951 by the Abbey of Our Lady of Gethsemani and renewed 1979 by the Trustees of the Merton Legacy Trust, reprinted by permission of Harcourt Brace & Company. Excerpt from *A Vow of Conversation: Journals 1964–1965* by Thomas Merton. Copyright © 1988 by the Merton Legacy Trust. Reprinted by permission of Farrar, Straus & Giroux, Inc.

This book is printed on acid-free paper.

A Forge Book
Published by Tom Doherty Associates, Inc.
175 Fifth Avenue
New York, NY 10010

Forge® is a registered trademark of Tom Doherty Associates, Inc.

Map by Mark Stein Studios

Library of Congress Cataloging-in-Publication Data

Green, Terence M.
    A witness to life / Terence M. Green.—1st ed.
        p.   cm.
    "A Forge book"—T.p. verso.
    ISBN 0-312-86672-0 (acid-free paper)
1 Irish—Ontario—Toronto—History—19th century—Fiction.
    I. Title.
    PR9199.3.G7574W58   1999
    813'.54—dc21   98-43614
                                                              CIP

First Edition: April 1999

Printed in the United States of America

0 9 8 7 6 5 4 3 2 1

For
David Danladi Luginbühl
Always remembered, always loved
Music forever
1974–1997

Acknowledgments

THIS BOOK, LIKE ALL OTHERS, IS AIDED BY ENTHUSIASMS AND kindnesses that bubble like springs around me.

Nancy (McLeod) Stobbs, Al and David McLeod, Betty McCaughey, Joe and Shirley Griffith, Mary Jane Barrack—all generously provided much valuable background. And my last conversation, in August 1995, with Joan McLeod was inspirational.

Elora deputy reeve and local historian Steve Thorning helped fill gaps.

In Ashland, Kentucky, booksellers Susan Thompson and Lisa Easter, and newspaper writer Cathie Shaffer, have all supported.

In Bardstown, Kentucky, Joe and Pam Zarantonello introduced me to Thomas Merton and the monastery at Gethsemani.

In Toronto, Ben McNally of Nicholas Hoare Books, Jean Sonmor of *The Toronto Sun,* Dr. Nick Loukides, and genealogist Jeff Stewart were all generous and helpful.

At Tor/Forge Books, Tom Doherty, Linda Quinton, Tad

Dembinski, Jim Minz, and Jennifer Marcus all made me feel like part of another family. Harold Fenn and his company have likewise been terrific.

Thanks to agent exemplary Shawna McCarthy; extra special thanks to editor extraordinaire David Hartwell, who helps me discover the shape and pace of my books with gifted insight.

Rob Sawyer, Andrew Weiner, Brian Dennis, Tom Potter, Bill and Judy Kaschuk, Ken and Judy Luginbühl—always there when needed.

But because this book is about family, ultimately it is my own family that I want to thank: my brother Dennis, my sisters Anne and Judy, my cousin Jacquie McCarthy; my cousins Jackie and Ernie Ongert and their son John Ongert; my Aunt Kitty in Arizona.

And right beneath my feet, tangled in my every move, the lights of my life: my own sons Conor and Owen, and my wife, Merle, who provide the world that makes everything, including this book, possible.

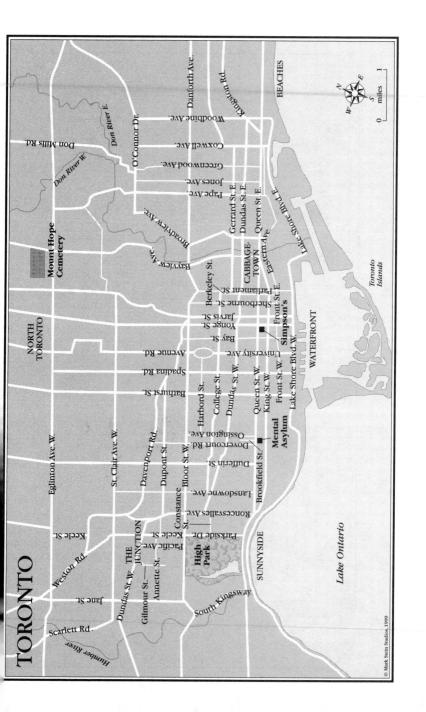

Peter Radey
1825–?

Julia Bunnet
1827–?

Martin Whalen
?–1845

Margaret Loy
182?–1917

Dennis Radey
184?–?

John Radey
1843–1906

m. 1859

Ann Whalen
1845–1920

Mártain Whalen
1842–?

Sarah
(O'Brien)
1860–1885

Margaret
(Dickinson)
1864–1945

Mary
(Rossiter)
1867–1952

baby boy
Radey
1870

Elizabeth
(McKenna)
1872–?

Bridget
(Trader)
1876–?

Teresa
(Curtis)
1878–1927

Patrick
1883–1884

Loretta
1885

Julia
(Johnson)
1862–1928

Mike
Radey
1866–1927

Ann
(Dickinson)
1869–?

Emma
(Manion)
1871–?

Kate
(Bedford)
1874–1940

Rose
(Kernaghan)
1877–?

Martin
Radey
1880–1950

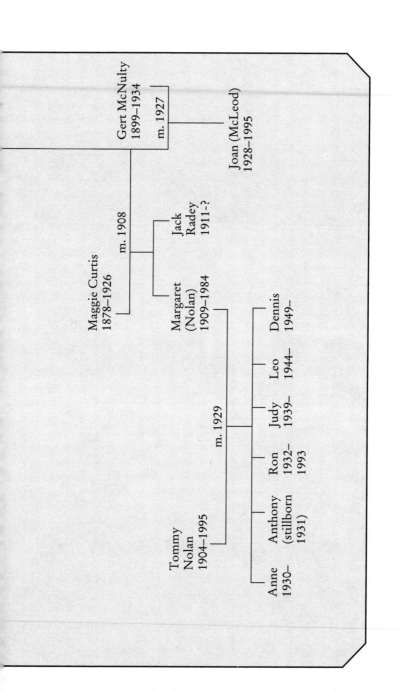

One

The door swings out upon a vast sea of darkness and of prayer. Will it come like this, the moment of my death? Will You open a door upon the great forest and set my feet upon a ladder under the moon, and take me out among the stars?

—THOMAS MERTON
The Sign of Jonas

IT BREAKS MY HEART TO SEE HER LYING THERE, WORN OUT, dying. But she is so happy to see me, and to see Jack, and this elates me.

And I am more than glad to see Jack too. I am renewed. It has been so long, so very long. And I have searched so far.

But Margaret. Oh, Marg. My princess. That this should happen to you. That I can do nothing about it.

My daughter. My first.

It is 1984. I am in the Women's College Hospital, Toronto. She is seventy-four. I look around, at the beds, the curtains, the tubes. The wrong place to die: a waiting game without dignity.

And yet she is older than I was when I died. I had the good fortune to die of a heart attack on the streetcar. But I was only seventy.

We are both too young. Everybody is too young.

I reach out, touch her face.

So does Jack, my son, whom I have not seen for more than fifty years. I do not understand how it is that he is here with me, nor why he is still a young man in his twenties, but I accept it as one of death's gifts. I understand very little anymore. Death has not taught me what I thought it might.

Margaret smiles, her eyes smile, knowing, understanding, and I think I might die again, just by seeing this. I know, suddenly, that there is not much more time. I do not know how I know this, nor what it means. And I have no idea what will come next.

One's life is supposed to flash before one's eyes when death comes. This is not true. It is no mere flash. It is much more complex. At least, it was for me. There is reflection. There is travel along the arc of space and time, back to source, ahead to destiny. I have been traveling for thirty-four years. I do not know how long it will last.

Something awaits me. Something. I know it. I feel it.

I am close. So close. Finally. Jack. Margaret. Here with me now.

It is part of the wonder.

Part of the mystery.

It was Christmas Day, 1950, a Monday—back before the subway was built, when the streetcars still ran up Yonge Street in Toronto and snaked on rails around the city everywhere, clanging, methodical. I was sitting in an eastbound car, on Dundas near Bloor, looking out the window, thinking about the eventual walk along Eglinton Avenue, about the icy wind that would burrow through layers of clothing— thinking about Dennis, my newest grandson, who would be two years old in March, and how much he would enjoy Christmas.

And it happened. I imagine that it has happened, and will happen like this, to millions, to billions, before and after my time—that it was happening to others even as it was happening to me. A complete surprise. So much surprises us, and yet so little should.

It was my turn to die.

I was coming to see you Marg, coming to spend the day. We hadn't spent enough days like this.

The pain filled my chest, but it didn't last long. Not really. I understand more now about time than I did then, and in reality it was merely a cosmic eye blink. I looked at the woman seated beside me, a stranger, said, "I can't breathe." My left hand clutched the chrome rail on the back of the seat in front of me, while my right hand instinctively squeezed the stone in my jacket pocket, the one given to me that day in the garden by the monk—that day in the sunlight. This stone is life, he had said.

I squeezed it fiercely. I thought of Joan, Margaret, Jack, then died.

Death has not been what I expected.

Not that I knew what to expect. I did have some concrete images in my head once, images that had blurred to vague concepts over the years, of a God, an afterlife—from being taken to church as a child, from my parents, from catechism lessons so many years ago. Nor would I have been terribly astonished if nothing at all had awaited me—a leaf fallen from a tree, becoming soil.

The streetcar shuddered to a stop, the woman next to me clutching my arm in fear and real concern. I heard a muffled hollering, knew confusion, as all that made sense slid away, like a morning dream. The conductor appeared beside me, and within seconds the car was being cleared of passengers. From far off, I heard him announce that the trolley was out of service and was proceeding directly, with all haste, to Western Hospital.

I remember looking out the window, from deep within me, through whirling, dying eyes, watching a flock of starlings rise up in widening circles from the pavement in a floating wave, a current toward the heavens. And as I watched, as I died, I became one of them, leaving my body behind, spiraling high above the street, the winter sky crisp, clear, seeing the interstices of streets below with an acuity of vision that I had never had before.

And then a kind of sense returned, a new order. This is what happens, I thought: a new clarity, a new vantage point.

I saw ahead to Yonge Street, north to St. Clair, farther to Eglinton. I tried to see Maxwell Avenue, running south off Eglinton, and the semidetached house that held much of what was left of my family, waiting for me.

Where you were, Marg.

Then I climbed higher, swooping with the flock, wondering where we were going, where I was going.

My name is Martin John Radey. I was born in Elora, a village some sixty miles northwest of Toronto, in 1880. I have been dead, as I stated, for thirty-four years. I accept what has happened to me, but I do not understand it. Perhaps acceptance is the beginning. Maybe understanding never comes.

I am the youngest of thirteen children who lived—eleven sisters and a brother. There were sixteen of us, if you count the three babies who died. We were all born in Elora.

Now we are all dead.

Back in 1950, as I soared high on the winds, the winter air searing the new, tiny lungs, I wondered, with a burst of incredulity and exhilaration, if I would see to my two brothers, who died as infants, or any of my sisters—my big sister, Sarah, who died before my fifth birthday, or little Loretta,

five months old, who died later that same summer of 1885—
my mother, my father, here in my new existence.

And Gert. Maybe Gert. Maybe Maggie. The thought startled me, exploding a rainbow of memories.

The flock circling me leaned in unison into an updraft, left
wings tilted downward, and as one we barreled north and
west. My heart, stopped forever in the body below us on
Dundas Avenue, had been replaced by one beating wildly
with wonder.

Ahead, the horizon arced and rolled as we left the city
behind, and below us the calm, brown and white winter
landscape spread far and wide in soft refuge. And then I re-
alized that I knew where we were going. We were going to
Elora. I was heading home.

Flying low over the fields around Elora, the snow disappeared. Time vanished. The past was here, to be felt, viewed,
examined.

I could see the old house on McNab, the post office in
Godfrey's shoe store on Metcalfe Street, the carpet factory,
the old bridge across the Grand. The Tooth of Time was
there, the stone fang jutting from the rapids beside the mill,
as always.

Suddenly: summer. Gardens with flowers, vegetables.
Elms, oaks, maples. The tannery, the brewery. The town hall,
the Dalby House, the sawmill. Cords of hardwood, piled
high. Horses.

And Father's shop, right beside Mundell's furniture factory. Where it used to be.

Through piercing avian eyes, above the earth, free, in
death, I saw things and places that I had forgotten, and a past
I never knew.

And above us, a single, hawk, wings motionless, circling,

entered a cloud. With new instincts, I watched for it, waited. It did not come out.

Father and Mother were Irish Catholics. They had liked to tell the story of how they'd come as children on one of the coffin ships—so-called because famine, cholera, typhus, diphtheria, and every other sort of blight sailed with them—that slid from Cobh, which the English then called Queenstown, in Cork Harbour. My mother, Ann Whalen, was one year old when she left Ireland in 1846. John Radey, my father, was three. The ships destined for North America docked at New York or Boston if they were headed to the United States; the cheaper passage was to British North America, up the St. Lawrence to Quebec City, then Montreal, before turning about and heading back across the Atlantic for another raft of human flotsam.

My father and his brother Dennis were in the arms of Peter Radey and his wife Julia, themselves twenty-one and nineteen. As with one-year-old Ann Whalen, her brother Mártain, and her mother, they took the cheaper passage; after the ordained quarantine at Grosse Isle in the St. Lawrence, all disembarked at Montreal, from whence they made their ways, along with so many others, by barge, steamboat, and lake boat, to Toronto. There was the special landing wharf, then the fever sheds at King Street West and John Street. That summer, more than eight hundred died in the sheds. Catholics mostly, they were buried in trenches in the graveyard at St. Paul's Church on Power Street. Even the bishop himself, ministering to them, died of cholera.

Eventually, it was by foot, wagon, and stagecoach over corduroy roads into southern Ontario, establishing themselves as best they could in the strange, new land. They settled, along with several other families, in and around Guelph for their first decade, then finally in Elora, when Da and Ma married and Da learned to be a blacksmith.

We were all born there. From 1860 to 1885, Ma had thirteen babies who lived, and three who didn't. I was born in 1880, the last survivor; I remember Patrick and Loretta, the babies who died in 1884 and 1885, and then there were no more. My oldest sister, Sarah, died of consumption, just before Loretta was born. Sarah, Julia, Margaret, Mike, Mary, Ann, Emma, Elizabeth, Kate, Bridget, Rose, Teresa, and then me.

I spent the first seven years of my life in Elora, until we left for Toronto in 1887. Moving to the city was an astonishing idea to me. I had been there only once, when I was four years old. We rode on the Grand Trunk Railway, to see Gramma Whalen, who lived in a strange stone building that Ma told me was called the lunatic asylum, and who did not know who I was. The building had a big shiny dome on top with a water tank in it that let everybody inside have running water, and Ma took me up the round staircase to the top of the dome to see it. I remember staring at the tank, picturing the wonder of water flowing into the rooms below like magic.

After twenty-seven years, Da abandoned his blacksmith shop, the soot and the fire, the ash settling everywhere about him. The city held the promise of husbands for his girls, husbands that they would never find along the banks of the Grand.

Two

1898
1899

1

THE ADVERTISEMENT IN THE AUGUST 10, 1898, EDITION OF *THE Toronto Telegram* newspaper reads *Wanted—Diningroom girl, Nipissing Hotel, 182 King East at George.*

"I'm going to apply for it," says Rose.

Ma looks at her, unsure.

"I can't keep working at the asylum. It's making me crazy. I'll be as crazy as them soon."

"Father." Ma looks at Da for help. He is smoking his pipe, rings of the sweet smell floating everywhere in the kitchen.

He shrugs. "I don't see the problem."

It is not the answer that Ma wants, and it shows on her face.

He knows this and continues. "It would make me crazy to work there." Then he looks at his wife. "It would make you crazy."

She presses her lips together, frustrated. Then: "But Gramma."

He shrugs. "Rose can't be expected to devote her life to that place just because Gramma Whalen is there." He pauses. "Let her go, Ann."

Watching them, Rose's face is torn. She has never taken such a stand before, and even if she wins it will seem like a failure.

Ma sits, holds her head in her hand, thinks.

It is September. I am working at the head office of Don Valley Pressed Bricks and Terra Cotta, 60 Adelaide Street East. I am eighteen years old, and with my first pay envelope have purchased a nut-brown, American-made man's fur felt hat, unlined, with Russian calf-leather sweatband, for two dollars at Simpson's, which I now place jauntily on my head as I head out the door.

It is five o'clock and it is Friday. The day is over. I am meeting Lillian at the Nipissing where Rose works. It is walking distance from both of our offices, and Rose will, as always, slide a bottle of Pabst beer our way.

Lillian is nineteen, has soft black hair, small lips, a filament of scar along her chin. She likes to touch my hands, my hair. I can think of nothing but her since we met at the St. Francis dance in the summer. The Cinematographe on Yonge Street last Saturday cost me fifty cents for the two of us, but since that time my head and loins have been whirling: she kissed me, her tongue touching mine.

I am surrounded by sisters. I am used to women. I think I understand them. But Lillian proves me wrong, proves me an innocent. Because I want her, because it seems possible to have her, my thoughts stop at her body, where they pivot and slue, caress and probe. I plot and scheme to be alone with her, to touch her, to let her touch me. I know about sin, about honor, about being a gentleman, but these things evaporate when we are together, and I am only what I am. And what I am is new to me, powerful and exciting.

* * * *

October, in the hayloft of the barn at Boyd's farm, off the Dundas highway, near the Humber, I lie across Lillian's softness and kiss her deeply. The rest of the church group is off on the hayride and will not return for an hour or more. We are not the only couple that has stolen away, but we are the only ones here, now.

I kiss the scar on her chin, her throat, touch her face, her shoulder, her arm. She holds me close, tightly, kisses me back, murmurs. She lets me open her clothing. I touch her everywhere, my mind fogged with desire. The knife-edge of frost hovers in the still air, our breaths misting slightly.

We make love. It is my first time, as it is Lillian's. I am thrilled, relieved, shaken, terrified. And Lillian, sweet Lillian. She clings to me, and I understand suddenly the weight of what we have done, what I have done. The aftermath of emptiness and confusion leaves me embarrassed. I think of my sisters, my mother. Women will never be the same, now that I know. And I think of Da, and glimpse his life as if through a dusty window for the first time. I had always wanted to be like my father, back in the blacksmith shop, back by the sureness of the forge, when sparks lit the air. But not now, not the way things are now. Now his life does not look all that enviable to my widened eighteen-year-old eyes.

"She expects me to marry her," I tell Mike. My brother is thirty-two, has been married seven years, has three children—Mary, Bill, and the baby, John, named after Da.

"You're too young," he says.

I shrug.

"Are you shaggin' her?"

"Jesus, Mike."

"Course you are. That's why she expects you to marry her."

"You're happy, aren't you?" I ask. We are sitting on the front verandah of his house on Gladstone Avenue.

"Mm." He pauses, thinks. "Happy's a funny word. I love my kids and my wife, if that's what you mean. But happy? I don't know about happy anymore. I don't know what it is." He looks around. "Half the time I'm scared. This place costs us eighteen dollars a month. Even a small furnished room with privileges would cost you twelve a month. Can you afford that?"

I shake my head. "No."

"Then what're you thinkin' of? Are you goin' daft?" But he smiles. "There are ways of doin' it without gettin' her pregnant, you know."

It is my turn to smile. I am enjoying my big brother's confidence, his knowledge that I am finally a man.

"You want to end up swallowin' Carter's Little Liver Pills every day like Da, complainin' about chest pains, stomach pains, every other sort of pain, while a horde of kids runs around your ankles?"

"Like you? Is that what you're saying?"

Again, he smiles. "You're too young. Don't get caught." He passes me a Sweet Caporal cigarette, takes one himself, and together we smoke them.

2

BECAUSE IT IS A BEAUTIFUL DAY, THIS FRIDAY, THE NINETEENTH of May, Lillian and I leave the Nipissing early while there is still light, walk north along George to Queen, then the half-dozen blocks east along Queen toward Lillian's parents' house in Irish Cabbagetown. The terrain of merchants and industry, thrift and enterprise, hope and ambition stands out hard and clear, the slanted sunshine flashing off glass facades:

Ball & Co., Men's Furnishings, Hats & Caps, 218 Queen East.

John Patton's Boot and Shoe Store, 224 Queen.

Wm. Tafts, Gents' Furnishings and Dry Goods, 226 Queen.

John J. Waters, Flour, Hay & Grain, 239 Queen.

George R. Fawcett, Men's Suits, 240 Queen.

C. R. Stong's Groceries, 252 Queen.

F. Belknap, Fish, Fruit, Vegetables, 260 Queen.

W. Muir, Hack, Coupe and Livery, 272 Queen.

J. R. Hancock, Suits Tailored, 275 Queen.

W. Mackenzie, Furniture, Stoves, New & 2nd Hand, 280 Queen.

R. A. Cardwell, Practical Hair Dresser, 282 Queen.

Geo. Hawkins, Fresh Meat & Provision Merchant, 288 Queen.

Robt. Fair, Hardware, 290 Queen.

A. A. McKay, Millinery, Shoes, 294 Queen.

Abbott's Meat Market, (Trading Stamps), 322 Queen.

E. J. Convey, Boots and Shoes, 330 Queen.

William Moore, Butcher, (Fresh & Salt Meats), 340 Queen.

J. W. Mogan, House & Sign Painting, 345 Queen.

Herbert O. Charlton, Furniture, Carpets, 347 Queen.

G. H. Moody & Co., Fresh Meat & Vegetables, 350 Queen.

The 9 Little Tailors Co. Ltd., 352 Queen.

R. W. Hislop, Baker and Confectioner, 356 Queen.

Geo. F. Moore, Conveyancing (Deeds, Wills, etc.), 359 Queen.

We turn south onto Power Street, where Lillian lives with her mother and three brothers. On our left is St. Paul's Roman Catholic Church, then the House of Providence—its spacious grounds and dignity housing the aged, the orphans, the destitute. Lillian lives across from it, atop Osgoode Dairy, at number 82.

In the tall grass by the woods beside the Don River north of Cabbagetown, in spring, sexually exhausted, clothes disheveled, Lillian and I lie entangled side by side. I roll over, shield my eyes from the sun, dizzy from the passion of the interlude. Then I drop my hand from my brow, close my eyes, and through sun-spotted lids I see that my boyhood is gone forever.

Three

Eternity is in the present. Eternity is in the palm of the hand. Eternity is a seed of fire, whose sudden roots break barriers that keep my heart from being an abyss.

—THOMAS MERTON
The Sign of Jonas

THERE ARE SO MANY ILLUSIONS. THERE IS THE ILLUSION THAT our life is all of one sweep, that it has a beginning, a middle, an end—that there is some shape that can be discerned. But instead of shape, I see now, there is texture, a surface composition mingled with a basic substance, woven from some primordial loom. Some of the threads intertwine tightly, some loosely, some are dead ends needing to be snipped. Many are soft, others coarse. They all wear with time, fraying, rotting with the rains and winds and the dryness of the sun.

We live several consecutive lives, and each time we look back on our previous life it is with wonder. Sometimes it is with fondness, other times with shame, but always with wonder.

Everything changes, replaced completely. And we move on, forward into the future, unraveling, shrinking, expanding, thinking that we are going somewhere.

How often have I stood with hand on doorknob, entering a room, and wondered how did I get here? Or stared out a window at my surroundings, listening to those with whom I live, and wondered how did this all happen to me?

And then we die, and the next surprise befalls us: there is more. And still, nothing is clear, except that the Day of Judgment is ongoing, in constant session, and that we are not punished for our sins, but by them.

The flock—my flock, I now think of them—was squawking, whistling, preening, in the branches of a great maple tree. I had no desire to disengage myself from them, and this intrigued me too. Why did I not fly off by myself?

I was not what I seemed, so I was convinced that they may not be what they seemed either. And when we sat there, resting, what did they await? When we flew, what did they see? The world, I know now, is mystical, not magical: mysteries that human reason cannot plumb.

I stared down at the city, through the hole in time, and saw the cleansing, the conflagration begin.

Four

Tuesday, April 19, 1904

The Queen's Hotel
Fine cuisine, courteous staff
210 boudoirs, 17 private parlors
Running water to all rooms
Telephone in lobby
Accommodation for 400 guests
Private garden, fountains
100 Front Street West, Toronto

"I'll be twenty-four years old in less than two months," I say.

My boyhood friend, Jock Ross, sitting across from me in the lounge of the Queen's Hotel, pours his second bottle of Carling's Ale carefully down the side of his tilted glass and nods. He watches the foam rise to a proper head before he smiles.

"So is that a complaint or a boast?" He sips the ale, sighs, sets it down, stares at me, eyes twinkling. "You're in your prime, same as me."

It is past seven o'clock and we have been sitting here since we finished work. "So what's going to happen to you and Nancy?"

Jock looks surprised. "What do you mean?"

"Isn't she on about marrying?"

He shrugs. "They always are. So what?"

"How do you put them off?"

"It's a talent. A gift. You should know that." He strokes the end of his moustache, still smiling.

I smile in return, sharing some imagined masculine confidence. Then: "Does it bother you?"

"What?"

"That you're deluding her."

"I'm not deluding her. She's deluding herself. I've promised nothing."

I sit back, thinking. Jock is an Orangeman, something that meant nothing to me when we were boys. Now it is an irony that we both view with amusement. Yet I wonder if there is some fundamental difference in our outlook that is rooted here.

My sister Teresa married Peter Curtis, a molder at Massey-Harris, last year. The wedding was enormous. Emma was maid of honor; his brother Fred, who works as an attendant at the asylum, was best man. The year before that it was Elizabeth who got married—to Jim McKenna, and I was best man, with Kate as maid of honor. There were one or two weddings a year it seemed. I danced with Peter's sister, Maggie, but now I cannot picture her face when I try.

"You want to end up like your father?" Jock asks.

Yes. No. I don't know.

"Not me. I've seen how my old man's been eaten alive with the responsibility." He sips his ale. "He'd give his eyeteeth to be here with us right now, doin' this."

I allow that this is true, but the argument still does not satisfy. "There must be more."

"There is. And I'm going to see Nancy later to indulge in it." A wink.

"Don't you want your own place, your own family?"

"Someday."

"When? When is it time?"

"Don't know. I just know it isn't time yet." He pauses, serious for a moment. "I guess you just know. I guess it depends on the woman."

"And Nancy?"

He frowns, thinks, dodges the question. "I tell you, Martin. It all scares the hell out of me."

"But living at home with our parents? It's got to end."

He concedes this with a nod. "That it does." Then he smiles. "Maybe next year." He empties the rest of the bottle into his glass. "And what about you and Kathleen?"

I smile, shrug. I know what he means. Lillian is a memory, as is Suzanne, Judith, others. Kathleen will join them, inevitably. And Harriet. Dear Harriet, back in Elora, my first girlfriend, my childhood love. Her head resting on her forearm, soft hair cascading across her wrist, her other hand laboring over the printed letters in the notebook on her desk in Miss Lecour's class. Gone like a wisp of smoke across the hills, from a time that I can scarcely comprehend.

And a new smoke wafts toward us from the present.

The wail of the sirens turns heads everywhere in the lounge, a mutter of curiosity floating among us.

The noise overwhelms, all talk stops. We wait, listening.

A man enters, tells one of the waiters loudly enough so that we can all hear that flames are rising from the roof of Currie Neckwear on Wellington, two blocks north of us.

Jock and I look at each other, drain our glasses, pull our coats and hats on, and head for the door. We are not alone.

How does this happen, this inferno? The newspapers the next few days will detail it relentlessly: the wind, the shortage of hydrants, the low-pressure water system, the errors in judgment, buildings with no internal firebreaks. The intestinal wonder of the modern high-rise—the elevator shaft—provides wind tunnel after wind tunnel, as flames roar upward through the chutes four stories at a bound.

After an hour of watching, our faces lit by the horrible glow, Jock and I return to the Queen's Hotel, sip another ale, subdued. We are numbed by both the weather and the event, but we do not go home. We remain near the flames, like moths, wanting to see how it will all play out. For now, the hotel is safe.

But it is not over.

Around 11 P.M., a blackened firefighter enters the lounge, tells us that we should vacate the premises, that we should go home.

No one argues. The lounge empties.

We venture back out into the unnatural heat and light, the sound of a nightmare unfolding mere blocks away. The flames have crossed Wellington, have moved south and east, leapfrogging to Brown Brothers' Stationery. As we watch, it and other once-dominant edifices collapse in upon themselves, become boiling ash-mounds that will not rest, a spectacle scarcely believable. A dozen or more buildings are ablaze. The heat cooks our faces, bakes the grimace into our mouths.

And still the radius grows. The firefighters work in the center of the maelstrom about us, beaten at every step, losing ground in inevitable stages. Flames rise higher than imaginable, a riotous Babel. Slowly, the hours like days, detachments pour in from Hamilton, then as far away as Niagara Falls, Buffalo. The wind whips our faces, whips the fires; the temperature drops, and strangely, snow begins to swirl.

It is 2 A.M. The news continues to spread. Troops and police jockey to maneuver the crowds. When the heat becomes too much for the firemen, they turn their hoses on nearby walls and stand angled beneath the ensuing spray, the suspended water drops like lit diamonds, adding to the dizzying visual. The downtown core is swollen with bodies. Looking upward, we see the roofs of buildings for blocks around, beyond any anticipated circumference of the fire, filled with onlookers seated on chairs, wrapped in blankets for warmth. And blankets again come into play—water-soaked ones, hanging from the top of the upper window sashes of the Queen's Hotel, to prevent the wood from catching fire. People fill every inch of street space, every step that affords a better vantage point, perch on every windowsill: a front-row view of the Horseman who rides among us.

We watch because we cannot draw ourselves away.

There are no words.

Then the Howland warehouse, stored with cartridges and dynamite, explodes, a volcano erupting, and we stand breathless. Plate glass windows shatter in icy showers. Burning walls topple, dust roiling upward. Against the orange of the fire and the black of the night, sparks from fallen electrical wires arc in blue crescents. From broken feed pipes, gas belches in mad jets high into the frozen air, as the earth splits and the pavement buckles.

The sky glows for miles and night disappears as we witness the apocalypse that levels our world.

Strangely, no one is killed. Twenty acres of our downtown world disappear, two hundred and twenty businesses. Things will never be the same. In the destruction we sense a new beginning, a chance to transform our world, ourselves.

The dynamiting of buildings rocks the city for days. It is two weeks before every small fire dies.

I never call on Kathleen again. I am changed. We are all changed.

Five

Wednesday, June 15, 1904

GRAMMA WHALEN SITS SILENTLY IN WHAT HAS BECOME HER chair at the kitchen table with us, her wide eyes focused on her plate, her mouth a small oval, her white hair pulled straight back. Since the fire, Ma has brought her to live with us. The very next weekend, in fact. First the asylum at Longue Point in Montreal, and now this, Ma says often, convincing herself. Two hundred people, including nuns, burned. Even though she cannot read, Ma saw the before-and-after drawings of the Longue Point asylum that were printed in *The Globe*. No place is safe, she says.

"Eat up, mother," Ma says.

Gramma Whalen ignores her, touches nothing.

Da and I pretend we do not notice. Da stares down into his dinner, slicing potatoes.

We are alone in the house. Gramma sleeps in Rose's old room. The girls have all married. It is what Ma wanted, but she seems to take little pleasure in the fact.

"Mother."

But Gramma doesn't look up. We don't know if she is thinking, dreaming, despairing, or merely resigned.

Ma gets up, goes over to her, cuts her vegetables, spoons some into her mouth, sits patiently beside her. Gramma chews absently. Sometimes she swallows, sometimes she does not. Today she swallows, and Ma sighs, relieved.

Da pushes his plate away, finished. He watches the two of them, expressionless. Then he lights his pipe, blows a stream of smoke upward.

Gramma watches it float aloft, disperse, disappear. She does not move.

Tomorrow is my birthday. I will be twenty-four years old. Nobody knows how old Gramma is.

Ma has made a small cake—chocolate, my favorite—which she sets before me at dinner's end. There are three small candles on it—white, red, and blue. Gramma stares at it, fascinated. There are only the three of us. Da is not yet home from work. Once again, I am the only man.

Ma strikes a match, lights the white one, does not light the other two. Then she sits back. "If you're lucky," she says, "the good Lord willing, you'll get seventy-five years on this earth. The white one is for the first third."

We watch the flame.

My glance slides in measured stages to the red one, the blue. The white one is a third gone already, wax gathering hotly at its base.

"Happy birthday." She pushes a gift-wrapped box across the table toward me—silver paper with gold ribbon encasing it. Gramma's eyes, unblinking, follow the movement of the package.

I smile. The ribbon slides off, the paper tears away, and I lift the cardboard lid beneath the glitter.

I am surprised.

First, I take out the straight-edged razor with the wooden handle. Unfolding the blade, I read "Killarney Razor" etched in its steel, and in smaller letters, near the hinge: "Marshalls, Argyle Street." I fold it, set it down, take out the shaving mug with the pattern of roses circling its wide lip next, lift out the brush inside it, touch its softness.

"The brush is made of badger hair," she says.

I can think of nothing to say yet.

"They were your father's grandfather's. Great-Grandfather Radey's. Your father's aunt had them when she died. They were with the few things they sent us after she passed." She looks at me. "This was almost fifteen years ago, when you were a boy." She pauses. "But now you're a man."

"Doesn't Da want them?"

"He wants you to have them," she says firmly.

I am moved. "Thanks, Ma."

We watch the candles. The white one is only a flame floating in a clear pool. Now she strikes another match, lights the red one. "The red one is for your next twenty-five years," she says, sitting back. "Your best years. Make them good ones."

I blow them both out. The blue one stands apart, unknowable. I look first at Ma's face, which is smiling, proud, then at Gramma's. Behind the wisps of smoke, Gramma's face is blank, as ever. But her eyes, I see with certainty and astonishment, are filled with water, staring into the smoke.

"Martin. Can you give me a hand?" Ma's voice, unusually abrupt, is coming from Gramma's room.

When I enter, my eyes scan the bedpan, the commode chair, the tubes, clean diapers piled high. The deadened air smells of talcum, of age. Gramma has slipped between the wall and the bed, wedged herself, and Ma is trying to wrest her loose. I lean across them, mother and daughter, and insert myself, holding Gramma's hand in assurance. Ma backs away, and I lift Gramma free, noting her weightlessness, feeling her frailty.

Gramma watches me, not taking her eyes from mine, a kind of wonder on her face. Fleetingly, I see my mother's face there, see Rose's, Bridget's, Kate's—then my own. The spine beneath my hand is a hollow keel, the breath, close to my face, castor oil. I touch her shoulder, feeling the bone beneath papery skin, beneath flannel. Gramma, I think. Gramma. I have never touched you before.

Suddenly, she is mine.

Da does not come home until past nine o'clock. Exhausted, he eats his dinner in silence.

I look at his shoes, covered with mud and cement, the heels worn down. He does not know it is my birthday, but I am not offended. He has never known any of our birthdays. And I never find out if he knows that I have his father's grandfather's shaving equipment, or if he really wanted me to have it, or if he even cares, because I never summon the courage to ask him.

He takes a Carter's Little Liver Pill, then lights his pipe. The blue smoke, strong with the smell of the life left in his lungs, fills the kitchen. None of us have any way of knowing that he will be dead within two years.

I remember the smell of the soot and fire, see the Grand River flowing wildly beneath us on the bridge, feel my hand tighten once again in the hair at the back of his head, watch him smile at the pleasure of holding me in his arms.

For unlike Gramma, I have touched him. But not for a long time. He has not been mine for a very long time. And soon, of course, it will be too late.

Six

The night . . . is a time of freedom. You have seen the morning and the night, and the night was better. In the night all things began, and in the night the end of all things has come before me.

—THOMAS MERTON
The Sign of Jonas

EVEN HERE, OUTSIDE OF TIME, THERE IS THE SUDDEN, THE UN-known, the dangerous. Without warning, plummeting like a stone from the clouds that scudded above us, a hawk—is it the same one I observed before?—fell to the top of the maple in which we were resting and plucked one of us from the uppermost branch.

Like an explosion, the sound of hundreds of wings beating. We lifted off in unison, a fleet of black specks of which I was a part, and swept across the city, heading blindly out over the lake, away from the clouds that could conceal such random fate.

My tiny heart was pumping fear, something I did not know I would feel again. And the questions flowed with it: who did the hawk take? Why? Will I ever know who these creatures about me are—or if they are anyone at all?

And it was real. In fact, it was surreal. I could feel it. There was no chance of a dream here, nothing of delusion.

We soared high, the blue waves far below us, finally arc-ing west, back toward the city. I saw the shoreline approaching, then Front Street, Dundas. We headed farther west, toward the Junction, exhilarated, and settled once again, a sinking black cloud, into a giant maple, where the sounds of relief, exhaustion, and the shrill chirps and squawks of life surfaced anew from the flock.

But we were one less. And I was uncertain why.

Life surrounded me. Yet in death, there was death still, a further echo.

I looked about, sifted through the years spent in the area—the rooms slept in, the faces staring from behind store counters, across tabletops. I saw mothers easing prams over curbs, fathers, thumbs hitched in their belts, striding beside them, bowlers tilted rakishly on their heads.

And then I held my breath. Oh, Maggie.

I saw Maggie, saw how my life really began.

Seven

1907–9

1

"MA AND GRAMMA ARE MOVING IN WITH MARY AND MI-chael. Into number thirty-eight."

Jock looks at me with interest. "When?"

"End of August." It is the seventh of June. "Since their oldest two married, there's only Francis at home with them now. He's thirteen. So they've got some room."

"And Julia and Oliver right next door?"

"That's right. And their five kids. Their youngest's got my name. Martin. He's eight."

"I can't keep your family straight."

"None of us can. Teresa and Peter Curtis live at thirty-seven Brookfield, Elizabeth and Jim McKenna at number thirty-nine." I laugh. "You know Kate married Jim Bedford last year—who works at Massey-Harris with Peter Curtis. Well, they've moved into number twenty-two." Once again it is Friday, the end of the workweek. We are sipping Bass Ale in the Nipissing Hotel, where Rose used to work, where I used to meet Lillian. They have remodeled the dining room, replaced the tables and chairs. I look around, knowing that I liked it better the way it was. "Ma needs help with Gramma. And my pay doesn't stretch far enough to carry the house and the three of us. Mary and Michael are doing well. Better, I should say."

"How's Mike—your brother Mike—doing?" He shakes his head. "See what I mean about the names? Can't keep 'em straight."

"Too many of us."

"Bloody right." He chuckles.

"Mike's got seven kids."

"Jesus. I'd lost track."

"His youngest, Kervin, six years old, is sickly. Mike's workin' his tail off to pay for medicine, doctors." I pause. "He's a good man. But he can't afford Ma and Gramma. Got no place to put 'em."

"What kind of name is Kervin? Irish?"

"Family name. Way back." I'm remembering the story. "My big sister Sarah married a fellow whose mother's maiden name was Kervin."

Jock's eyebrows rise slightly.

"Sarah died a long time ago. When I was a kid. It's Mike's tribute to her in a way. Her memory."

Jock seems sobered by the story. Then: "Mike still on Gladstone?"

I nod. "Still there."

Almost a minute passes in silence. Then he asks: "So?"

I meet his eyes.

He waits.

"So I guess it's time. Got to get my own place." I shrug, take another sip of ale. "I can't cook, you know. I'll probably starve."

I expect Jock to tease me further about my future helplessness, but instead he is quiet, looks thoughtful, then tips his own glass to his lips, places it back on the table before speaking. Finally, he says, "What about getting a place together?"

"Who?"

"Us. The two of us."

It is a new idea to me. I say nothing, digesting the thought.

"Time I got out too," he says. "Couple of old bachelors like us might have a pretty good time of it. What do you think?"

"Interesting." The picture of it grows slowly in my mind, a seed planted, roots spreading.

"We could save money by splitting the cost of a place."

I have no money saved, never have any money saved, live pay envelope to pay envelope, even after almost a decade at Don Valley Pressed Bricks.

"Very interesting." I smile.

We order steak and kidney pies, another ale, consider possibilities. I feel liberated. As much as the unknown frightens, it also excites.

"The Catholic and the Orangeman." Jock smiles back at me. We are conspirators. We have saved ourselves. Like the remodeled room in which we sit, we too will have a new veneer. The future opens up anew.

Uplifted by beery collusion, heartened by the balm of a June evening, I amble along the south side of King toward Yonge Street. This is the old city, spared the fire of '04. Across the street, at number 66, I see Brown Bros., Ltd., the stationers and bookbinders where I once interviewed for a job that I did not get. At number 46, the Canada Life Building towers upward. It, too, has a place in my memory. Inside are the offices of Hearn & Lamont, Barristers, Solicitors and Notaries, in room 47, where I also have been turned down for clerical work.

In the street, amidst the other single carts, a horse-drawn streetcar—"Toronto Street Railway Company" emblazoned on its side—heads sedately westward, on a line that will eventually take it just south of the lunatic asylum, which, in spite of Ma's direst fears, is still standing. And above the clopping of horse hooves rumbles the sound of an open two-seater "Northern" auto. Other heads turn to stare. Seated high, a man and a woman smile proudly, squinting into the setting sun.

From my inner jacket pocket I take a Havana Eden Perfecto, one of my treats to myself, and stop outside the elegant new King Edward Hotel while I light it. Perhaps, I think, smiling, Jock and I will be able to afford a celebratory drink here soon, when we acquire our new accommodations.

Puffing it into life, I watch a young woman stop by the double-sided water trough opposite me by the curb, dip the cup on the chain into the basin facing us, and, tipping her head back, drink. In the weakening sunlight, my eyes are drawn to the sensual line of her throat, the way her fingers splay away from the metal vessel at her lips. And as I listen to her footsteps fade away, fasten my gaze on the slimness of her ankle as she disappears, I know that there is something else that I need and must have, something that I am missing profoundly.

Rounding the corner onto Yonge I head north, thinking I will walk the four blocks to Queen, then catch the streetcar home. At 97 Yonge, I stop at Chas. Rogers & Sons, Co. (Ltd.), Furniture & Upholstery, and read the sign in the window:

LOWEST PRICES FOR CASH
BEDROOM SUITES
BRASS BEDSTEADS
PARLOR SUITES

MANTELS & GRATES
DINING SUITES
TILES & FIRE IRONS
SPRINGS & MATTRESSES
HALL STANDS
ETC.

I will need furniture if I have my own place, I think, suffused with a sudden influx of realism. The thought bothers me, but it cannot fully penetrate the glow of the ale still coursing through my veins. Subdued only slightly, I shrug the thought off, move on.

Two doors north of Adelaide, at number 113, I halt once more, this time outside the windows of Samuel Corrigan, Merchant Tailor (established twenty-five years). Clothes are a weakness of mine, a small vanity. They are a major reason why I cannot pay "lowest prices for cash" for even a spring and mattress from Chas. Rogers & Sons. Having never needed furniture before, I have never developed a curiosity about it, have no sense of its worth. I have lived for myself, have always been good to myself, always tried to dress and groom like a gentleman.

The sign is perfectly stenciled:

DIRECT IMPORTER OF SELECT WOOLENS
SCOTCH TWEED SUITINGS
$15, $16, $18, & $20 UP

The temptation for something smart, something with which to celebrate my new independence, grows delicately in my brain, as it has so often before. I have never needed much of an excuse.

But Samuel Corrigan, Merchant Tailor, is closed.

Simpson's, I think. Simpson's or Eaton's. Large department stores. They'll be open Friday evening. And Simpson's, for whom Mike still works, delivering goods to all parts of the city, is closer, less than two blocks north.

Pulling the brim of my hat down, I set off.

At Richmond Street, I enter Simpson's corner doors, wander onto its wooden floor, feeling small beneath the high ceilings, beneath the weight of the six stories atop me. The escalator, the flat-step moving staircase, rolls noisily upward in the distance. Once inside, I take my hat off, still unsure what it is that I want, and stand staring down long, brightly lit aisles, hypnotized as always by the baskets holding customers' change and receipts clicking along overhead on trolley wires.

Business is modest. A lady stands to my left at the counter displaying scarves and shawls, holding one aloft for inspection. To my right are a series of mannequin torsos, brazenly displaying ladies' corsets. Flustered, I drop my eyes to the hat in my hands.

And it is here, in my own hands, that I get an idea.

The men's hats and ladies' millinery counters are side by side, and I lean tipsily on the glass, staring at the array of sumptuous headwear. There is a woman bending beneath the counter, stowing a box away, who does not know that I am here.

She straightens, brushes her hands on the front of her skirt, and meets my eyes. The face that greets me is frail, perhaps somewhat older than mine, the eyes large. Her hair, tied at the nape by a white ribbon, is swept up one side and across the top of her head so that it falls in a soft roll across a high forehead. The mouth curves down at the corners in a way that is both sad, and to me at this point in time, particularly alluring.

"Can I help you?"

Suddenly, I am the one who feels frail. And foolish. I do

not know what I want anymore. My desire to adorn myself, to play the dandy, blends into something else much more mysterious.

I place my hat on the counter. "I was thinking of a new hat," I hear myself saying.

I have always thought the fur felt hat, with its Russian calf-leather sweatband, to be a fine piece of manhood. In fact, I purchased it at this very place, almost ten years ago, with my first pay.

But now I am not so sure. The realization surfaces that being surrounded by females of all kinds is no guarantee of understanding them, and I am taken aback.

It lies on the counter between us, more than a hat, and remarkably less. Her eyes drop down to study it, then rise once more to meet mine. She is wearing a white, high-collared blouse with a pin at the throat, which falls in ruffles at her bosom. Her hands, I now see, have small veins on their backs. The nails are short, well kept.

I know her from somewhere, but cannot place where.

"I see," she says. Then a finger touches the brim. "It is an old hat. Looks like it has been worn well."

I have never thought of it as an old hat, or worn, well or otherwise. Through her eyes, it transforms.

"I bought it here," I say.

"An older style. We have new stock. A great deal. What did you have in mind?"

"I don't know," I answer honestly. Things have shifted. I realize that in some minute way, I am not the same man who wore the hat into the store. He is gone. I have replaced him. Who is she?

"Silk hat? Opera hat?"

I lean forward on the counter and study the signs hanging behind her head, but in so doing, unthinkingly, I come too close to her. I do not understand this until I see her face contort slightly, realize from her expression that she has smelled the ale on my breath, and has judiciously backed away.

"I'm sorry," I say.

She says nothing.

I am mortified in a way that is new to me. "I've just come from—"

I stop.

"I'm sorry." I pick up my hat, nod. I turn and leave. I feel her eyes on my back as I stride down the aisle toward the door. I am careful not to betray myself further, not to embarrass myself with a stumble, a false step.

Sitting on the streetcar, traveling home, I am in a daze. I see nothing but the mouth turned down at the corners, the hair rolling across the forehead, the pin at the throat. I see the hat between us on the glass counter.

The next day, Saturday, I return, stand at a distance from her counter, beside a table that announces: BRACELET, 35¢; BEAD PURSE, 59¢; SHAWL, 50¢. I have no plan. I only know that things were not right, and now, in the clear light of day, I have to fix them. The floor is bustling with energy, with people who need to be in a place like this after managing the routines of their lives for another week, and it occurs to me that I am one of these people.

But she is not here. Another woman is displaying wares to a customer on the glass counter that stood between us last evening.

I swivel my gaze throughout the room, fixing on faces, scanning. Then I look back at her counter. The woman here now is younger. In a way that I do not understand, she is less than the woman I saw yesterday.

Above her head, I read the sign OSTRICH AIGRETTES FOR 75¢, GOOD ASSORTMENT OF COLORS.

I approach, stand with fingers touching the dark wooden edge of the glass counter. When she notices me, I try to think of something to say. I ask to see the men's fur cap encased beneath my hands. The woman, younger than me, than her, very pretty, soft features, complies, passes it to me, smiles without showing her teeth. I touch it, turn it over in my hands.

"This one's astrakhan. We have them in half Persian lamb, nutria, beaver, German otter... They're only three dollars and fifty cents. Good value." The voice is pleasant, friendly.

"It's very nice." And it is. I let my fingers probe its exotic mystery, its suppleness. Its softness. "Thank you," I say. "Thank you for showing me." I hand it back.

She continues to smile.

I cannot buy it from her. She does not tell me that my own hat is an old one. Her mouth does not curve down at the corners.

That night, Saturday night, I meet Jock downtown and we make the rounds. We drink ale, eat sausages and eggs and pigs' feet in beverage rooms with sawdust on the floors, spend an hour with two women named Diane and Caroline, whom we meet at the Nipissing, neither of whom I can picture clearly in my mind the next day.

But it is not the same for me as it has been in the past. It is not the same. My mind is elsewhere.

Her face. I know her.

When I stumble in the door past midnight, I know that something is amiss. All the lights are on. I hear voices from an upper bedroom.

I pause at the foot of the stairs, clear my head, listen.

* * * *

63

The priest is standing at the foot of the bed. He has just conferred the last rites on Gramma. She lies there, tiny, covered with a checkered quilt to her waist. Her feet are small hillocks beneath its weight. Someone has wrapped rosary beads about her hands. A clean blue nightgown is tied tightly at her neck.

There is blood in her stool, Ma tells me. Ma does not know what this means. They have called the priest instead of a doctor, which, somehow, does not surprise me.

On the bedside table is the bottle of Lourdes water, more than twenty years old, that I have been told Father Owen gave to Ma when Sarah died. The only other time I have seen it is when I was six years old, when Rose was sick, that winter, when Ma, her eyes fierce with fear, rubbed it on her chest, praying for her cough to disappear.

Extreme Unction. Father Owen. Miss Lecour.

The memory of St. Mary's School—of catechism lessons—back in Elora floods back, like the Grand River, wide and powerful. I stand in its midst, an obstacle to be eroded, the Tooth of Time.

Gramma's eye sockets, lips, ears, hands glisten with the holy oil, with forgiveness of sins she has never committed, could never commit.

Her eyes roll toward me, watery, fasten tightly. Her mouth opens in a small *o*.

No sound.

But she is alive. She is alive. Still.

Da did not receive the last rites. I saw him myself, that day, before he was washed.

He died at work, after eating the tomato sandwich that Ma always made for his lunch, beside a road excavation bed that he had just carefully lined with crushed gravel. They say that he caught his foot on the pedal of the steamroller, fell and struck his head on the metal side, hung twisted from one leg. They could not find Ma, but the men told me they knew my name and where I worked from listening to Da brag about me, so a man in a faded checkered shirt and suspenders, sad eyes, and a floppy moustache curving over a thin mouth, his broad-brimmed hat gripped in soiled hands, came to my work and told me and took me there to see him. He was lying on a grass boulevard beside the sidewalk, covered with a tarpaulin. Work had come to a halt, and the twenty-one men on his crew stood about silently, leaning on shovels, rakes, brooms. One sat astride the giant steamroller, his face a blank. I said nothing as I looked down at him. The death certificate would list the cause of death as a fractured skull, and make up his age, because he had always shaved years off to keep jobs. I remember the mud and cement caked on his shoes, the gray dust of his labor on his hands.

And watching Gramma, I know, suddenly, that like Da, when my own time comes, I will not receive the last rites either. And because Da did not receive them, I know, too, that I do not want them.

I wonder if this is one of the things it means to be a man. I wonder about the possibility of redemption.

Gramma does not die that night. Before dawn comes, the priest has left, but we are still with her, exhausted, not knowing what we want.

When I fall asleep, finally, in the early morning, I dream the dreams of the drunk, of the dazed, of the ones who have seen, however briefly, their own abyss. I dream of Sarah, my sister, buried when I was a child, see her dying, her white dress bloodied, her eyes frantic.

I dream of a lone hawk, soaring high above me, high above us all.

*   *   *   *

"Gramma," I say.

She looks at me, says nothing. We are alone.

It is the next day. Sunday. Ma has gone to late mass with Mary, Michael, and Francis.

"I'm glad you're feeling better."

I remember the night I touched her, lifted her. Now, I put my hand over hers, cover it, hold it, feel the thinness of its liver-spotted surface.

She looks down at our hands in wonder. Then she looks up at me, makes the *o* with her mouth, studies my face intently, tilts her head, and I feel her fingers tighten on mine.

"Would you like a cup of tea?"

Her face begins to shake.

I set the two cups of tea on the bedside table, beside the Lourdes water. Propping the pillow, I slide her into a sitting position. Touching her again, I think.

She weighs nothing.

"I put sugar and milk in yours too." I lift it to her lips, hold it steady. She drinks, a few drops spilling on her chin. When I place the cup back on the bedside table, she blinks at me and her lips part, but no sound comes out. She studies my face carefully.

"I met a woman," I say, hearing my thoughts come to life.

She listens to the words, watches my mouth.

"I went to see her again, but she wasn't there." I sip my tea, sit back, relax. "I think you'd like her." I smile.

Her silence is profound for me. I think of all the women's voices that have surrounded me my whole life, contrast them with Gramma's quiet calm.

I hold the cup to her lips once more, watch her fists clench and unclench.

*   *   *   *

When Ma returns, I ask her. "What's Gramma's name?"

Ma looks at me. "What do you mean?"

"Her real name, her full name." I have never asked before. I do not know why I have never asked.

She is preparing a stew for our dinner. The carrots have been chopped, lie scattered on the wooden board. Turning from her work at the kitchen counter, she faces me. "Margaret," she says. "Her maiden name was Loy." She frowns. "She married Martin Whalen. My father. You're named after him."

"Where was she born?"

"Ireland."

"Where in Ireland, though?"

"The Whalens, the Loys, the Radeys," she sighs. "Your father was born in county Kerry. I was born in King's County. Kerry's the wild county, green and rolling, near the sea. The southwest. King's County is more in the center, farther east. It's farming land. Southwest of Dublin. Northeast of Cork." She wipes her hands on her apron, lifts her chin, stares at me, silent, in thought.

"How old do you think she is?"

Her eyes shift to the wall behind me as she answers. "I've wondered myself, many a time." A pause. "I'm sixty-two. So I'm told," she adds. "Born in eighteen forty-five. How old does that make her?"

I don't know. I don't know what I am supposed to know. "Was she old or young when you were a child?"

"What do you mean?" Her eyes move back to me.

"You know. You were fifteen when Sarah was born, thirty-five when I was born." Thirty-five sounds so old to me as I say it. Maybe, I think suddenly, I should not have mentioned Sarah.

But she smiles.

I wait.

"There were just the two of us. Me and my brother. His name was Mártain, too." She pronounces the name with its Irish lilt, and I hear the old language, hear it sing. "So you see, there's a Martin in each generation."

Then she pauses, seems to be remembering. "She was young," she says. Then: "Did you know that her name, Loy, is the Irish for shovel?"

I shake my head, say nothing, just listen.

Her lips move, as if to say something, as if to complete the thought. But she says nothing else aloud.

"Father died in Ireland, shortly after I was born. Mártain was three. Eighteen forty-five. At the beginning of the famine."

Ma sits at the kitchen table as she speaks; I stand by the window.

"That's why there are only the two of us." A pause. "He choked to death on a piece of meat. We were all there, even me, wrapped in a blanket in a box. It was dinnertime." Another pause. "Mártain used to tell me how mother screamed and screamed. He was too little to do anything. He used to say that he remembered it vividly. He just cried. He was scared."

I have never heard this before, have never asked. I am stunned.

Ma is quiet for a minute. Then: "That was the beginning of the end for Mother. They say she was never the same after that. By the time we left Ireland, the next year, her mind was going. We had been evicted. We had nothing. Everybody had nothing. There was no food. Nothing. I try to imagine it." Ma stops, hesitates, then: "She wasn't as bad as she has been since you've known her. But she wasn't able to make the decision to emigrate. Uncle Liam made that decision, and put her and Mártain and me on the ship. He was Mother's brother. He did most of the looking out for us the year after Father died." A pause. "Liam's dead."

The story hypnotizes me. "What happened to Mártain?" I have never met him, have barely heard his name over the years.

Ma looks at me. "Last I heard, he was out west somewhere." She turns her head to look out the window beside me. "It's been years." Her voice can scarcely get the words out. "I don't know what happened to him," she says.

That night, I go in to see Gramma before going to bed. She lies there, the Lourdes water beside her, looks at me. We look at each other.

"I met a woman," I tell her.

She opens her mouth, startled.

"You'd like her." I place my hand on hers.

She squeezes it tightly, frantically. Her eyes study my face.

"I know her from somewhere." I am touching her.

2

ON MONDAY, AT TWELVE NOON, I LEAVE WORK PROMPTLY, knowing that I do not have much time on my lunch hour. Within ten minutes, I am inside the doors of Simpson's Yonge and Richmond entrance, within the crackle of mundane trade and commerce—in a place that is beginning to feel quite comfortable.

The first thing I notice is that the sign has been changed. Now it reads: OSTRICH PLUMES 12 & 18" LONG, WELL CURLED, DUCHESS STYLE—REGULARLY 2.25 TO 3.25 FOR $1.48. The second thing I notice is that she is here, beneath the sign.

*　*　*　*

I stand, watch, but do not approach. She is busy serving a customer, a woman. But I do not notice the customer in the same way that I notice her. I see the high-collared blouse, the high-waisted skirt, the hair rolling across the forehead. The pin at her throat, I now see, is heart shaped. And her mouth does indeed curve down at the corners, full, soft. I have seen her before, somewhere.

Watching her, not daring to approach, I cannot fully grasp my fascination. My need.

My desire. My fear.

From various points on the floor, in a secret world, I watch until I must leave, note her movements, her patience, her mannerisms. Then, to my own surprise, I go back to work without letting her know that I was there.

In the offices of Don Valley Pressed Bricks and Terra Cotta, the events of the afternoon flow by me, dreamlike.

My lunch hour the next day, Tuesday, is a repeat of yesterday's. In Simpson's, I float about the floor, as casual as a bumblebee visiting daisies on a summer afternoon, yet I never take my eyes from her. I watch her move, sigh, smile, sag, touch her hair, straighten the items on the counter. I watch how she rubs the back of one hand with her fingers, unthinkingly, as she passes the time, waits for the next customer. She wears no rings.

But I am still afraid to talk to her, and I am uncertain why I am afraid. Yet even being this close feels right. For now.

When I stand in front of her the next day, at precisely 12:15 P.M., she smiles hesitantly. Then I see it in her eyes. She remembers. And her eyes tell me that she is trying to remember something else, the same thing that I am trying to place.

The smile falters, returns.

"Good afternoon."

She returns the courtesy. "Good afternoon."

"I was in here last Saturday."

"I remember."

"I'd like to apologize."

"I don't see what for."

"For everything."

She says nothing.

"Please forgive me."

"Nothing happened."

"I did not behave like a gentleman."

"On the contrary, you were a perfect gentleman."

"Only after the fact."

"Sometimes after the fact is the perfect place for courtesy, when it has been missed in the first instance." She stares at me. "Second chances are important."

I feel warmed by her largesse. "Thank you."

She smiles. When she does so, the downturned corners of her mouth disappear, and to me, she is radiant. Her eyes drop to my hands. "You still have your old hat."

"I do. I do indeed. What do you recommend?"

She shrugs. "Depends. Formal or informal. Formal, I'd think you'd suit a Homburg. Slightly curved brim, dent in the crown."

I watch as she stretches to take one down from a shelf on the men's side, see her laced shoe with the almond-shaped toe peek from beneath her skirt.

"If you're thinking of something informal, you'd be wanting a boater. Straw. Summer's coming." She looks at me, intrigued. "Either'd suit you."

"I have a boater," I say. Everybody has a boater. I do not add that it, too, is rather old.

She smiles quizzically. "Then the Homburg."

"Hmm." I consider. Then I see that her fingers are touching the brim, and my mind is set. I must have it.

I take it from her, watch as her fingers slip off. Turning it over, I run a hand within its white silk interior, along the richness of the leather sweatband. I try it on. It is a perfect fit. How did she know?

"I'll take it."

"You look smashing." And she smiles. Smiles the radiant smile.

In a mood of exuberance, my new hat boxed beneath my arm, just before I exit the store, on an impulse I stop and pick up a stainless steel thermos bottle. I am not sure why I am holding it. No one I know owns a thermos bottle, with its promise of hot or cold drinks anytime one wishes.

I roll it in my fingers, surely a sign of good things to come.

One dollar and ninety-five cents. Another celebration.

It seems a splendid thing. I pull two ones from my wallet, buy it, stroll grandly through brass and wood and glass doors, feel the warmth of June on my hands and face, seeping through my suit.

I pour the hot tea from the thermos into the cup that serves as its lid and hold it to Gramma's mouth. Her lips grope at its rim, drink noisily. I wipe her chin as I take it away.

"It's called a thermos," I tell her.

She looks at me, head trembling ever so slightly, unsteady on her thin neck. The skin hanging loosely from her jawline is like talcum powder, a soft corduroy that might melt at the touch. Her mouth forms the *o*.

I take her hand, place it on the side of the steel container, let her feel its smoothness, its strength.

"Now you can have hot tea anytime you want."

She looks from it to me and back again.

"I spoke to her today."

She stares at me, a bird trembling.

"She sells hats in Simpson's. I can't get her out of my mind."

Gramma reaches for the cup cradled in my hand, a finger slipping into the warm liquid. I hold it to her mouth, watch as her eyes roll back in her head, as she swallows in gulps.

Steadying her as she drinks, I think, suddenly: Margaret. Margaret Loy. I picture her screaming in the kitchen of a thatched cottage, a baby in a box, while a small boy cries on the dirt floor beside her.

In Simpson's the next day, I watch her again, working up my nerve. But I do nothing about it. I cannot think of a believable ploy to approach her. I need an excuse, but can think of none.

Life stalls, eddies.

Her face, her eyes, her mouth.

"I don't know what to do, Gramma."

In a surprising move, she reaches across and touches my face, my lips, running her fingers along my cheek.

I let her touch me. I let her probe for the source of the person sitting beside her. Then I take her hand in mine, hold it, feel the fingers curl about mine, feel it relax.

How, I wonder, did this happen? How did it become Margaret Loy and me? It has come out of nowhere. And it occurs to me, just as abruptly, a sudden insight, that perhaps everything comes out of nowhere.

"Help me," I say to her.

The fingers tighten. I sit there. Together, wordlessly, we plot.

I wait until Friday, until the end of the workday, guessing that she will be working Friday evening, as she was last week, as I now imagine she does every week as a matter of course. She sees me coming across the floor, smiles that curious smile, waits.

"Good evening."

"And good evening to you." Her eyes glance at my head. "And how is the hat?"

I am sporting the new Homburg, feeling resplendent. "Couldn't be better. One of my finer purchases." I touch the brim. Her hands, fine boned, rest on the glass counter.

I ask it. "Would you enjoy a cup of tea? Some coffee? A drink after work?"

A beat. Several beats. What I have sensed before is true. She is older than me. I feel it fully now. This has been part of the mystique, I realize slowly—my inability to be more worldly than her. Something I perceive dimly as her experience. Her hesitation is the interval of assessment, of intuition, of decision.

But her answer is kind. And warm. "What a pleasant idea," she says.

My spirits soar.

"And how would we go about this? I don't finish until nine." She waits.

"Does someone come to pick you up?"

"No." She is smiling broadly now, understanding the game, the necessary moves, but the smile is still laced with reserve. I am being studied carefully.

"Have you had dinner?" I ask suddenly. Maybe there are more possibilities.

"Yes. An early one. At five."

I shrug, return to my original idea. "I could have a bite to eat. Do some shopping. I'd be back at nine to meet you here."

The corners of her mouth uplift into a grace. "Why not?"

And I am happy. It is that simple. "My name is Martin Radey."

She nods, continues to smile, bemusement and recognition crossing her features like a cloud's ground shadow on a sunny day.

"Margaret Curtis." The eyes staring into mine are hazel, and with her name I now know what she knows. We have indeed met before, at my sister Teresa's wedding. We danced, once, the day her brother Peter married my big sister Teresa. I have not seen nor thought of her since. "Call me Maggie," she says, carefully, imparting an intimacy, bonding us to that vanished moment. The word is both shadow and sunshine, hope and loss, and infinite possibility.

"And what is it that you do now, Martin Radey?" She has appropriated the pouring of the tea. I watch her hands, one holding the curved handle, the other pinning the lid to the teapot so that it does not tumble off. We are at a table in Bowles' Restaurant, at the corner of Queen and Bay.

"I work in the receiving department at Don Valley Pressed Bricks and Terra Cotta."

"And where is that?"

"Adelaide Street East. Not too far from here."

"Is it a good job?"

I shrug. "It's a job."

"But is it a good job?" She places the teapot carefully at the side of the table, wipes the spout with a napkin.

"It's the only job I've ever had. The only real, full-time one. I've been there for almost nine years."

"Then how do you know if it's a good job or not?"

I sip my tea, consider. "What do you mean?"

"To know if it's a good job or not, it seems to me that you'd need to have something to compare it to."

I listen to her, but I am mostly staring at her mouth. "I see what you mean."

"Do you?" The odd smile again.

"I think so," I say. Even her voice, its cadence, has my attention.

She sips her tea. I watch how her lips, lightly flushed, glisten as she sets her cup back into the saucer. "Did you know," she says, "that the National Council of Women called for equal pay for equal work at its assembly earlier this year?"

This catches me off guard. I am uncertain what she is talking about. "No," I say. "I didn't know that."

She smiles. "Have you heard of the National Council of Women?"

I watch her. "I confess. I haven't." I feel suddenly foolish. How could I not have heard of it? What have I been doing?

"Most men haven't," she says.

I do not want to be most men. I am not sure if we have made a strong start together. I still see the unshaped girl in my mind. This is unsettling, in complete opposition to what I would have hoped, even dreamed of. I ask: "And how long have you worked at Simpson's?" And then, boldly, I add, "Is it a good job?"

"Those are two questions, Martin Radey—"

My name. From her lips.

"—and I'll have to give you two answers."

"I'm in no hurry." It is true. I will listen to her for hours, if she will let me.

"I have worked for Robert Simpson's since the end of the Boer War. Since nineteen oh two. Five years now. Just shortly before Emmeline Pankhurst founded the National Women's Social and Political Union." She watches me. "You do not know of Mrs. Pankhurst, do you?"

Her skin is truly soft, and she is really quite tiny. "No," I admit. "I don't."

"She's determined to have the women's right to vote."

"A suffragette."

Her face lights. "Yes. I'm glad to know that you are familiar with the term."

Finally, I think. Finally. I have pleased her.

"Bills on women's suffrage have passed second readings in the Commons five times since eighteen eighty-six but have never proceeded beyond that stage. Someday, it will happen. Already, there are five states in America that have achieved suffrage for women. Wyoming has had it since eighteen sixty-nine. In eighteen ninety-three Colorado followed suit. And now Utah, Idaho, and Washington have fallen in line. Our day will come, even here."

I am speechless. I stare at her in wonder. Slowly, I raise my cup to my lips, savor its abundant warmth.

"I've scared you, haven't I, Martin Radey?"

"Not at all." I hold the cup aloft. "You fascinate me. You don't scare me."

"You're sure?"

"Quite."

"I have a habit," she says, "of mounting an occasional soapbox. It scares men off."

"I must be tougher than most."

"Glad," she says, "to hear it." The smile, still tinged with the hint of irony, relents, seems to accept. We have apparently crossed a bridge.

She pours herself a second cup of tea. "To answer your other question: yes, it is a good job. I know this because I have had much with which to compare it. Before I was at Simpson's, I worked at Townsend Steam Laundry and at the Princess Laundry. I also worked briefly at Reedow Caterers, out in the west end. We catered weddings, dances, banquets, conventions, and the like. I even worked for the Davidson & Hay, Limited, importers and packers of Kurma Tea. We sold it to grocers in pounds and half pounds, black or mixed. Do you know Kurma Tea?"

"No."

"British. Very nice. This," she says, indicating what is on the table, "is not Kurma."

"Mm."

"And then, just before joining Simpson's, I worked for Creelman Brothers Typewriter Company."

"Really? I've seen it. It's on Adelaide, right near where I work."

"You're absolutely right. It is." She smiles. "You should've come in to see my typewriter demonstration."

"I should've."

"Men cannot handle them. Perhaps it is their fingers. I think it is more basic than that. Women and typewriters were made for each other."

"I guess I haven't given it enough thought."

"I learned quickly. I was their demonstrator. Did you know that there are probably over one hundred fifty thousand lady typewriters in America and Canada today?"

"I had no idea."

"And an office girl can make ten dollars a week. More than twice what she could earn in a laundry or kitchen."

The salary shocks me. It is more than I make.

"So you see, Mr. Radey—"

"Martin."

She stops, smiles. "So you see, Martin, I have a very good idea of whether my job is a good one or not."

"I'm glad you have found a good job."

"But it isn't that good." She sips.

"I thought you said—"

"That I could tell a good job from a bad one."

"Ah."

"My job is acceptable. That's a long way from good."

What she says rings true for me. Much of my life has been acceptable. Yet it, too, has been a long way from good.

Through the restaurant window, I watch a string of black birds—feathery, puffed pearls beaded along the roofline of a storetop across the street.

Maggie Curtis follows my gaze. "They're European starlings," she says. "There were a hundred of them released in New York's Central Park back in the 1890s. Now they're everywhere." She looks at me. "Immigrants," she says. "Like us."

I stare at her, into her assuredness, wanting, against hope, for this to be the crossroads we all await.

"Do you like to read?"

"Newspapers. I like to read the newspapers," I say.

"Books. Do you read books?"

"Not many." I think. "A biography of Napoleon, when I was in school. Mother had a Booth Tarkington novel at home that was given to her. I started it. It didn't interest me. I read some of *House of the Seven Gables*. It was around the house. Quite imaginative, but not quite my cup of tea." A pause. "I guess I'm not much of a reader."

"I'm reading one now called *Sister Carrie*. It's about a girl who goes to Chicago and becomes a man's mistress. When it first came out it was deemed immoral." She smiles.

"Where did you get it?"

"Eaton's. I bought it."

I have never bought a book, and have trouble digesting the idea.

"It's like a breath of fresh air," she says.

* * * *

"Why did you want to meet with me, Martin? Did you recognize me?"

"Only when I heard your name." Why, indeed. I cannot articulate it. I am not sure myself. I am driven. "You're a lovely woman," I say. "Who wouldn't want to meet with you?"

"Nonsense."

"Pardon?"

"I am not a lovely woman. In point of fact, I am somewhat unlovely. I have to watch my waist, especially since I refuse to wear a corset, and I am astute enough to be fully aware that I am unremarkable in most other ways as well. I have no money, I come from a common, workaday family as you well know, and I am far past my prime."

"Maggie—"

"It is true." A pause. "Do you know where I was born?" She does not wait for an answer, and I do not know the answer anyway. "Burnhamthorpe. A village of one hundred people, at Dixie Road. It has a blacksmith shop, wagon shops, a shoemaker shop, a general store, and a post office. Farmers from the north stay overnight at the Puggy Huddle Hotel at the Second Line east on their way to market in the city. I come," she says conclusively, "from nowhere."

"I don't know what you're talking about." And for a moment, I do not. This strange self-assessment has derailed me.

She waits a few seconds. "How old are you, Martin Radey?"

"I'm twenty-seven." Close enough, I think.

"I am twenty-nine. Most women my age have been married for a decade, and have a brood of children. Do you know that life expectancy for a woman is fifty-one? For a man, forty-eight?"

I am stunned. She is moving too fast, cutting away layers of the game. "I did not."

"I read it in the newspaper. But because you are a man, you can father children until you die, while I, on the other hand, have seen my prime years disappear. So don't tell me that I am lovely. Or that I am desirable. Or any other of that romantic claptrap."

"But," I say, I implore, "it is true."

She tilts her head on an angle, places her fingers against her cheekbone, purses her lips, contemplates me anew, as if another layer of skin has been peeled away, exposing a rawer, simpler truth.

"It is true," I say. Again.

And then we are silent. We sip our tea.

Maggie pours me a second cup. I let it warm me, do not want it to end.

She lets me see her home. We ride comfortably on the Queen car, pointing out stores, landmarks, making small talk, listening to the clop of hooves. I point out Brookfield Street, where I live, as we pass, before realizing that she must know of it from Teresa and Peter. At Dufferin, we transfer to a northbound car that wends its way onto Dundas, where she lives, she has explained, with her parents and remaining unmarried brother and sister.

It is far past where I have to go, but I do not mind. In fact, I want to delay returning home.

At her front door, I doff my Homburg, hold it in my hand, ask it. "Are you working tomorrow?"

Her eyes meet mine. Hazel. Older than mine. Already, she has shown me that she is much more than I have ever known in a woman. "As a matter of fact, no. I have one Saturday a month off, and tomorrow is the one."

"Do you have plans?"

"One always has plans."

I am disheartened.

"But nothing that cannot be adjusted."

The space between us seems immense. I have not touched her.

"Can I see you tomorrow?"

A beat. A decision. "What would we do?" she asks.

I don't know. I don't care. "Have you seen *The Great Train Robbery* at the nickelodeon?"

"I have. Yes."

"So," I admit, "have I."

She smiles.

"We could go for a picnic. It is June." She does not appear unlovely to me, especially the smile, the corners of her mouth turned up with promise, with hope. When she does not protest, I forge ahead. "To the Island, perhaps. The sky looks clear. It should be a nice day."

I cannot believe that I have done this. I cannot believe that I have set myself up so blatantly for disappointment. I am standing here with this woman who has drawn me like a magnet to a far corner of the city, for whom, at this moment in time, I would do anything, and do not know why.

I hear only the night crickets.

She reaches, takes my hand in both of hers. I feel the small bones, see, even in the faint lamplight from the street, the fine veins on their backs.

She knows, I think. Knows me. Maggie.

"That sounds very nice."

When I get home, Gramma is asleep. But I stop by her room, step inside, and tell her anyway.

The following Monday, I buy my first book. I buy a copy of *Sister Carrie* at Eaton's. That night, by gaslight in the kitchen, I read:

Here was neither guile nor rapacity. There were slight in-
herited traits of both in her, but they were rudimentary.
She was too full of wonder and desire to be greedy.

3

190 Michigan Ave.
Detroit, Mich.
August 30, 1908

166 Crawford St.
Toronto, Ont.

Dear Martin & Maggie,

Your wedding was a blast! I am still recovering. Maggie's parents served up a feast fit for kings, and Maggie, Martin certainly
showed good sense when he decided to hang onto you. You have
my permission to box his ears anytime he shows a lack of appreciation. I expect that you two are comfortably nested in your
new quarters and happy as pigs in poop right now, and well you
should be.

I was right back at work within two days and we haven't let
up since. We've got a power-driven conveyor belt at the plant now
on which the car frames are set and we managed to average 93
minutes for each car assembled! And if you think that's fantastic
you should hear the rumors buzzing around about how we'll soon
have a new car assembled every ten seconds of the working day and
the Tin Lizzies as we call them will only cost a few hundred dollars
apiece. I hope it happens soon as I want to own one just like everyone else. Instead of looking after all that I did previously my job
now is only to fasten on the right rear wheel. Walter Norton beside
me bolts the mudguard brackets to the frame. At the tenth station

the engine is dropped in and the body bolted on and it's ready to roll. All of Detroit is talking about us.

Wish I could have given you a Tin Lizzie for a wedding present, then you could have tossed a few camphor balls into the gas tank for pep and driven us home. Cora and I think of you both often, and Cora says hello to you both and thanks you for including her in your reception as she had never been to Toronto and was quite impressed. The heat surprised her even though it was August as she said that she thought Canada would be much colder.

All the best for now to you two and remember what they say about the Ford, that it is the best family car as it has a tank for father a hood for mother and a rattle for baby.

> Your vaudevillian Best Man,
> Jock

> 166 Crawford St.
> Toronto, Ont.
> Sept. 21, 1908

98 Portland Ave.
Rochester, N.Y.

Dear Emma & John,

A small thank you from Martin and me for the wedding gift of the beautiful glass bordeau lamp, but your presence at our wedding was the real gift. I hope the trip home was pleasant and that we will see each other more often in the future. Martin is indeed fortunate to have such a sister and brother-in-law.

> Fondest regards,
> Martin and Maggie

166 Crawford St.
Toronto, Ont.
Sept. 21, 1908

Monastery of the Precious Blood
118 St. Joseph St.
Toronto, Ont.

Dear Sr. Bernadette,

I'm sorry to have taken so long to respond to your letter and gifts, as they deserved a more appreciative thank you. But things were so hectic leading up to the wedding and settling in to our new flat that I only now feel that I can make the time. The scapulars will be worn fondly and Martin's watch lining is grand. He sends his thanks as well.

I trust all is well with you and hope that we shall see you soon. I remain

Your good friend,
Maggie

---

190 Michigan Ave.
Detroit, Mich.
July 25, 1909

166 Crawford St.
Toronto, Ont.

Dear Martin,

Thought of you yesterday (today is Sunday) when we were down at Detroit Beach on Lake Erie and we saw all the families with kids playing there. Let me know the minute the baby arrives, Cora and I will pop a champagne cork that you might hear all the way from Detroit! My friend Walter Norton has managed to buy a Tin Lizzie

and he and his girl Mary Alice and Cora and I drove down to
spend the day at the beach. Walter let me drive for a bit, we didn't
get stuck even once. What a ball!

I was offered a transfer to Ford's Walkerville plant across the
border near Windsor but turned it down. They've been turning out
Model C, K, N, R, & S since '04 there but now that they're gearing
up to turn out Model Ts they need more men. Want me to give them
your name? Interested? A family man like you could use the money.

Like the song says, Toot Your Horn, Kid, You're In A Fog.

Jock

FROM   MARTIN RADEY
        166 CRAWFORD STREET
        TORONTO ONT
        22 AUGUST 1909

TO   JOCK ROSS
        190 MICHIGAN AVE
        DETROIT MICH

MARGARET MARY RADEY BORN AUG 21 AT 6 LB 6 OZ
STOP MOTHER AND DAUGHTER DOING FINE STOP FA-
THER SMOKING A BIG CIGAR AND TOOTING HORN IN
A FOG STOP POP THAT CHAMPAGNE STOP

DADDY MARTIN

Eight

It is strange awakening to find the sky inside you and beneath you and above you and all around you so that your spirit is one with the sky, and all is positive night.

—THOMAS MERTON
The Sign of Jonas

Now, in 1984, Margaret lies before me in the hospital bed, dying, and I know, without knowing why, that the death within death that I have witnessed in the treetops, in the sky, will come to me shortly, a hawk falling from the clouds, and that all this will end. That is why I am here, a final stop on my ethereal trip, loosed from the flock of lost souls with which I travel. And looking at Jack, my son, I now know that he too is dead, that Margaret is seeing us exactly as she last remembered seeing us, and I am filled with a longing and a sadness and a joy beyond understanding. That is why I am here in my seventy-year-old body and why Jack is smiling, in his prime, handsome in his early twenties.

Words are not needed. We all understand. It is what happens. It is how we close the door.

Then Jack does a remarkable thing. He hands me a small stone, smiles. I am breathless. I close my hand over it. Oh Margaret. Oh Jack. I look at them both, see babies, then children, see everything good that I managed to spoil, and silently ask for their forgiveness.

Nine

1911
1912

1

ON APRIL 30, 1911, JACK IS BORN. JOHN FRANCIS RADEY. MY son.

When Margaret was born, my heart melted. With Jack in my arms, my chest swells with a pride I never knew. Babies, both, but so different. Margaret, so easy to please, so eager to please in return, Jack pulling away, creating his own space. I sense this immediately, instinctively. A son and a daughter. I am the luckiest man alive. Yes.

We are in a new flat on Lansdowne Avenue—the second floor of the middle house in a row of three. All is wonderful, yet all is chaos. Margaret always slept at reasonable times, is perpetually good-natured. Jack is the opposite. He cries at night for hours, leaving us exhausted for days, weeks at a stretch—exhaustion such as we have never known. Margaret did not prepare us for this. Is it the difference between boys and girls? We do not know.

Maggie's eyes are red with the burden. I live in a strange

isolation from her as she withdraws into herself, not needing me, needing only sleep.

She sleeps with the children.

I think of my father, how I suddenly understood him once I had been with a woman, with long-forgotten Lillian. Now I understand him again, more fully. I understand his life, what he gave. I close my eyes and see him eating quietly at the end of the table.

Typhoid fever is what people are talking about in the city. The downtown area reports hundreds of cases, and we are glad we live near the west end. Yet I travel every day into the city center and listen to the talk, hear the reports. The city adds chlorine to the drinking water, explaining that this chemical will kill the disease, that the germs are in the water.

I drink it, taste the difference, fill empty milk bottles, seal them carefully by wedging cloth in the necks, take them home to Maggie and the kids in a shopping bag. When I cross Yonge Street the two miles from Front to just north of College are aglow with six thousand new streetlamps, like a fairy tale, pumped to us from the giant generating plant at Niagara Falls.

The city ablaze with electric light, bottled water that will spare us. Miracles abound. Things are not so bad.

On Saturday I treat myself to the Harrison Baths at McCaul and Stephanie Street. It is heaven. A thirty-minute bath, complete with showers and a towel: ten cents. Refreshed, I stroll toward Yonge Street, cross to the south side, and enter 57 Queen West, R. A. Caldwell Hair Dressing & Shaving Parlor ("Razors Honed"). After the twenty-cent haircut, the chair folds back and I lie there, eyes closed, amid perfumed and leather scents, as my face is lathered and scraped. When I am asked if I would like my neck shaved as well, I say yes, why not, I would, aware that it will add another five cents to the ten-cent shave, but I do not care. I close my eyes again, wish Jock were here, wish we could go for a glass of ale afterward.

I stand at the Yonge Street wharf and watch as the new *Trillium* sails toward the Island. The ferries, I realize for the first time, are flowers. *Primrose, Mayflower, Blue Bell,* and now *Trillium,* the largest. Flowers on the water. Dreams.

Fire has consumed the past. I sift through the ashes, quiet, try to envision the new order. I can see the rebuilt Hanlan's Point amusement park, see the strings of colored lights even in the daytime, even from this distance. But it is not the same. In '04, the city, in '10, the Island. The Figure-8, the Scenic Railway, the old Mill, enveloped in flame. The House of Fun, the Penny Arcade, all there when Maggie and I watched diving horses, all gone, replaced by something new, something I can only see while standing here at a distance, something I do not know.

The *Trillium,* white, cuts the blue water.

Flowers. Dreams.

Flames in the city. Flames on a birthday cake. Blue water. A blue candle, burning slowly.

"Listen to this," Maggie says. She folds over the copy of *The Toronto Star* newspaper as she reads. "The life expectancy for a woman is fifty-three years. For a man, fifty-two."

I have heard numbers like these before, but have forgotten them.

"It used to be fifty-one for a woman, forty-eight for a man," she says.

"We're gaining."

"We're not." The newspaper is folded again. "And it says here that the number of children that a healthy woman living in wedlock should have is ten."

"Who says?"

"The Vice Commission of Chicago."

"What is that?"

"I don't know. Some fool commission of men who have no idea what it is to be a woman." She looks at me. "Don't you think two children is enough?"

I think of my father, of thirteen children. "I don't know," I say.

I see her face, the new lines.

She folds the paper, says nothing, breathes rhythmically.

2

THE TOPIC CHANGES AT WORK. JUST BEFORE MIDNIGHT ON Sunday, April 14, 1912, the world's largest floating vessel, the White Star liner *R.M.S. Titanic,* strikes an iceberg in the Atlantic and sinks within three hours. Of her 2,206 passengers, 1,503 drown. The list of names of those dead does not sound like anyone I know: a colonel, a novelist, an artist, an editor, a millionaire book collector.

In the days that follow, we discover that of the 703 who are picked up by the *Carpathia,* several are from Toronto. A fellow named Arthur Peuchon from the Island's Royal Canadian Yacht Club, the RCYC, is soundly criticized by the local press upon his arrival home for not adhering to the time-honored code of women and children first. We talk of little else for weeks.

I think of Maggie, of Margaret, of Jack. I think of drowning so that they may live, of the honorable thing to do.

On a Saturday morning in July, Maggie and I are standing in the summer sun outside the new Woolworth's store at the northwest corner of Queen and Yonge, Jack in her arms, Margaret clinging to my hand, as the city's only motorized fire truck howls by us, bells clanging. Jack's attention is complete, Margaret is enraptured.

I pick small, dark-haired Margaret up in my arms so that she can see better, watch her face as her neck cranes, as the truck disappears, her eyes beautiful, big. Jack is so excited small bubbles sprout on his lips as he tries to sputter his enthusiasm.

I smile, holding her, watching him, seeing Maggie wipe his mouth, his chin. Seeing my family.

August swelters. In our new three-room flat on Lansdowne Avenue we lie awake nights, bathed in sweat, the air still.

Jack cries. Margaret crawls in with us. We wait for morning.

The Toronto Star responds to the summer's heat and humidity by announcing a "swat the fly" contest, with cash prizes for the most dead flies produced. On August 19, two days before Margaret's third birthday, more than three million flies are turned in to the newspaper. A neighbor, Beatrice White, wins fifty dollars for producing 543,360 flies, weighing more than two hundred pounds.

On Saturday evening, the street throws a party for Beatrice, who shows everyone the dozen wire-mesh traps in her yard that she used to catch the flies. Molasses, she explains. That's the key. Beatrice is a celebrity. We delight in having her among us, previously unaware of her ingenuity. Maggie and I drink beer, wander from porch to porch, exchanging pleasantries, complaining about the heat wave, Margaret and Jack in tow. When they finally fall asleep on Mrs. White's unpainted wicker verandah chairs, we carry them home, put them to bed. They lie there, beads of perspiration on their upper lips, their brows, skin perfect, ours.

Perhaps it is the heat, the beer. I touch Maggie the way we used to touch each other, and she softens, is there for me. Finally. It's all right, she says. It's a good time of the month, my cramps are just starting. It's safe.

I hear her as if from a distance, wish she would stop worrying, planning. I kiss her mouth, her neck, tremble. It's been so long. So long. I touch the small of her back where I have pulled her blouse loose. Her hands cup my face. She breathes into my mouth.

It is October, the heat long gone, the trees yellow, red, when Maggie, folding the newspaper in her lap, says, "Norway has given women the right to vote."

I look up from my own piece of newsprint, say nothing. I barely know where Norway is. I picture Norwegian women, tall, blond, emancipated, casting ballots, discussing politics.

I think of the children. I try to understand. I try.

In November, Maggie reads to me from *McCall's* magazine. *The Ladies' Home Journal, Good Housekeeping, Life, Collier's.* Maggie reads everything she can get her hands on. "There is an Italian educator named Maria Montessori who has a fascinating article in here about educating children."

"Margaret is only three," I say.

"That's not too early, according to her. Even Jack."

It is evening. The children are asleep. I take a cigar from my vest pocket, roll it between my fingers.

"She speaks of educational toys. Says children can learn from toys, from color, from proportion."

I think about this. "What kind of toys?"

"Numbers, letters, pasted on cards—alternate rough and smooth paper—so that the child learns to distinguish between the smooth and rough texture, without realizing that the letters and numbers are also being learned."

I strike a match, puff the cigar to life. I think back to Elora, to St. Mary's School, remember no toys. All that comes to mind is Dewey, my rag doll, clutched while I slept.

"They become familiar with forms long before they know any purpose for them. She calls it sense training."

I listen, fascinated, think about Margaret and Jack, and through the blue smoke see the dream called the future, see them in wonderful brick houses with fine clothes and shoes, their families about them, healthy, educated, all reading books.

On Friday, December 20, instead of going directly home with the small brown envelope the size of a playing card that holds my weekly pay, I trudge back and forth in the snow between Simpson's and Eaton's, riding the escalators to the toy departments. I buy a circular alphabet board made of metal and fiber, twelve inches in diameter. It has eighty letters and characters and a drawing slate in the middle and costs me $1.39. I buy wooden alphabet blocks, a set of jacks, an Erector set. A toy milk wagon, twelve-by-four inches, with red-spoked wheels, twisted wire loop handles, rubber tires, and metal wheels, costs me fifty-nine cents. The front wheels turn. And then, picturing Margaret with it in her hands, I buy a toy piano, eleven-by-sixteen inches, with fifteen keys and a lithographed front consisting of birds in a tree and the word "Symphony." The $2.98 price is more than a day's pay, and dizzy with the excitement, I have to stop the wild spending.

But before I leave, on the main floor of Eaton's, thinking of Maggie, I buy a perfume atomizer for thirty-seven cents and a manicure and toilet set for $1.69.

Nine dollars, I think. I have spent more than nine dollars. It is Christmas, I tell myself. Jack and Margaret will be excited. And swaggering through the snow to the streetcar, picturing their reactions, their faces, I am euphoric.

"We don't have nine dollars to spare," Maggie says.

"It's Christmas."

"What will we do for the groceries, for the rent?"

"I'll borrow some."

"From who?"

I do not know. "From mother. From Mike."

She shakes her head, touches her brow.

"I have money," says Margaret, who has been listening. She reaches into her pocket, pulls out a nickel. "Uncle Mike gave it to me." Her English is perfect, her eyes dark and round.

I think of the atomizer, its rubber squeeze ball, its scrolled surface, of the manicure and toilet set, combs, mirror, brushes, scissors. Jack is clinging to my leg. I reach down, pick him up. He plays with my tie, my collar, my ear. Margaret holds out the nickel.

FROM   JOCK ROSS
         190 MICHIGAN AVE
         DETROIT MICH
         23 DECEMBER 1912

TO   MARTIN RADEY
         DON VALLEY PRESSED BRICKS AND TERRA COTTA
         60 ADELAIDE STREET EAST
         TORONTO ONT

$10 ENCLOSED STOP PAY ME BACK 5 AND SAY MERRY XMAS TO THE KIDS AND BUY A TREE AND SOMETHING FROM US STOP GETTING MARRIED IN THE

SPRING WILL WRITE WITH DETAILS STOP GET READY
TO COME TO DETROIT STOP

SANTA

3

I POUR TEA FROM THE SILVER THERMOS INTO MY CUP AND SIP
it slowly. "Margaret is the only one that I make happy," I
say. When the words are out, they astonish me because I
realize that they are true, yet I have never thought them before.

Propped up against her pillow, Gramma listens, stares.

A long pause: the trickle effect of what I have uttered runs
through my veins, opens doors. "I disappoint everybody
else."

Gramma opens her mouth. I lean forward with her tea,
help her drink.

"Even though he's still a baby, Jack has no interest in me."

Gramma looks at me.

"Maybe when he gets older."

We sit quietly for a while.

"I think Maggie expected more."

The cup warms my hands.

"I don't know what they want."

Her mouth makes the *o,* her eyes soften, and I think,
maybe, she understands.

I dream that Jack and I are on a wooden dock by a lake when
Jack slips into the water and beneath the surface. I dive into
the water, hold my breath, search, but cannot find him. I dive
again and again, deeper, lungs bursting, but he has sunk out

of sight. I know that he cannot last much longer without air. I am frantic. The water is black. He is gone.

A moan breaks from my chest. I wake up sweating, heart pounding, Maggie holding me by a shoulder.

"You were dreaming," she says. "A bad dream."

"I lost Jack." I am panting. "I couldn't find him. I couldn't save him."

In the darkness, she strokes my head, my brow. "You're all wet," she says.

I am cold. Jack, I think.

Jack.

Ten

We must always walk in darkness. We must travel in silence. We must fly by night.

—THOMAS MERTON
The Ascent to Truth

THE HAWK TOOK ANOTHER.

A burst of feathers, soundless. We erupted from the field, an explosion of black dots, knowing that death was among us, our movements random, swaying, spurred by the primal flight from extinction.

To the south, then east, headlong, for hours.

Into another node, another loop. Fog.

Suddenly, below us, the St. Lawrence. May 29, 1914, and the *Empress of Ireland,* rammed by the Norwegian collier *Storstad,* sank out of sight completely in fourteen short minutes. We settled into trees near the shore, listened, watched. One thousand fourteen people silenced. The hush, the mist, shrouded us. As before, we had fled the hawk only to encounter the cleansing of fire, the finality of water, always.

The *Titanic,* women and children first. Jack, in a dream, disappearing beneath dark waters, my lungs squeezing, dying.

Through the fog and the curved horizon that was the future, I now could make out the blurred shape of troops that would sail to England down this same river, across the Atlantic, and knew that if I soared high enough I would almost be able to glimpse them plunging down muddy embankments at Ypres, the yellow gas falling, heavy as it tumbled into the trenches, into their lungs, into their hearts and the hearts of their families forever, replacing the fog.

The hawk we have fled was clean, simple, pure. It was right.

The world, both large and small, was in madness.

We lifted off, moving, again.

Eleven

1916
1917

1

IT IS 8 P.M., JANUARY 18, 1916. MAGGIE IS TELLING ME ABOUT Manitoba's Nellie McClung, who has succeeded in attaining the right to vote and hold office in her province. It is seven months since the sinking of the *Lusitania* by a German U-boat and the drowning of 1,198 people, whose grave, strangely, is Cork Harbour, the port from which mother and father sailed in 1846. Farther north, in Dublin, in three months the Easter Rising will occur, taking with it thousands more lives, ending in the court martial and execution of fifteen men, leaving more than one hundred thousand in the city on public relief. In Brooklyn, New York, Margaret Sanger is being arrested and jailed for opening a birth control clinic and dispensing information. The Parliament buildings in Ottawa will be destroyed by fire within a month. In two months, the legal drinking of alcoholic beverages will cease for eighteen years in Ontario, and stores will sell off their stock before the deadline. D & W Special Whiskey will go for seventy-five cents a quart. A walk down Dufferin in the evening and a glance along Liberty Street reveals shell casings like giant empty gray pods lining both sides of the street as far as one can see, higher than a man's head, overflowing from the munitions factory that is staffed mostly by women. Six months from now 624,000 Allied troops will perish during the offensive at the Somme, and fourteen months later, American president Woodrow Wilson will take the United States into the war in Europe, the war in which everyone has a friend a brother a cousin an uncle.

There is a knock at the front door and we hear Verna from downstairs talking with someone. Then there are footsteps on the stairs and Maggie and I turn expectantly at the sound. Margaret, six and a half, and Jack, not yet five, both wrapped in a blanket, close to the stove, stop talking. The circus characters carefully arrayed on the sofa beside them, figures of wood, enameled in colors now faded and chipped, are ignored. I lay my cigar in an ashtray, the blue smoke slow to rise in the cold winter air of the room, fold my newspaper. It is wartime. We have no telephone. A knock on the door in the evening is seldom a good thing.

When I open the door, it is Mike, my brother. He has been to our flat only twice before. Our lives, like so many others, have separated, somehow, inevitably, without our being aware of it.

His face is ashen, sunken, his eyes blank.

Dear God, I think. Oh, God.

Both Bill and John, his two oldest, are overseas, Irish sons fighting England's war.

But then he speaks, standing there in the doorway, says: "It's Kervin, Martin. He's dead."

I don't know what I'm hearing. Kervin. He is not at war. He is here, at home. He is just a boy. Mike's youngest.

Mike comes forward, puts his arms around me, puts his face on my shoulder, holds me tightly. I feel the coarseness of his hair against my cheek, feel him trembling, am filled with his pain. My brother. He cries, and I hold him, pull him closer, afraid to let him go.

Jack and Margaret are silent, still.

Mike is seated, a cup of hot tea in his hands.

"What happened?" I ask.

He shakes his head, shrugs. Mike is fifty, his hair thinning, his face gray. "It was his heart, they say. He wasn't strong enough." He looks at me. "Heart failure. He was only fifteen."

I remember Kervin, coughing, sick. "Have you told Ma?"

He shakes his head. "No," he says. His head continues to shake. Then, again, "No."

Maggie and I glance at each other, then at Jack and Margaret, and cannot speak. Without words, we have said it: we cannot imagine this. It is impossible to imagine.

At 5 P.M., Friday, March 17, 1916, Peter Sterling, the owner and president of Don Valley Pressed Bricks and Terra Cotta, calls me into his office to tell me face-to-face what he has been telling others all day. He is seated behind his desk. "Sit down, Martin."

I sit.

"You know what I'm going to say."

"Yes."

We are quiet for a moment. He is writing on a piece of paper. Peter Sterling, an Orangeman, a Lancashire man, took a chance on me, hired me when no one would hire an Irishman, even one born in Canada. I have always thought of him as a model of decency, of fairness, of Presbyterian sobriety. He wears a blue suit, a red tie, his hair white, his glasses thick. I have never seen his wife, his family, although they say he has two grown sons who work in Chicago. I do not know him well at all. We live in different worlds.

"It's true. I've sold the company and will be retiring. The company will cease to exist as of the end of the month. The new owners will bring in their own people. I'm not a young man anymore." He pauses. "How old are you, Martin?"

"Thirty-five. I'll be thirty-six in June."

"And you've worked here a long time."

"Almost eighteen years." Half my life, I think.

He writes something on the piece of paper. "And you have a wife and two children."

"Yes."

He nods. "What will you do?"

I look into a corner of the room, away from his face, puzzled. "I don't know," I say. I am one of twenty-four employees. I do not know what any one of us will do.

He folds the paper on which he has been writing and slides it into an envelope. It lies on the desk between us.

I look back at his face, realize he is not really seeing me, that he is somewhere else, distracted. He is thinking of his life, not mine.

He picks up the envelope, hands it to me.

I take it, rise, shake his hand, leave.

> *Don Valley Pressed Bricks and Terra Cotta*
> *60 Adelaide Street East*
> *Toronto*
> *March 17, 1916*

To Whom It May Concern:

The bearer of this letter, ___Martin Radey___, has been in my employ for the past ___eighteen___ years. During this period

I have always found him to be honest, and reliable, and I have no hesitation in recommending him.

> *Sincerely yours,*
> *Peter Sterling (President)*

In the envelope, with the letter, are five ten-dollar bills.

I walk north to Gerrard, then east. It is a long walk, but I know exactly where I am going. When I reach the southwest corner of River Street, I enter the Shamrock Hotel, seat myself in a corner, order a pint of Guinness and a Blue Union Label cigar, and slump into the shadows. It is, after all, St. Patrick's Day, and there are only five more days until the temperance forces will close down the Shamrock, the Winchester, the Nipissing, the Rupert, the Dominion House, the Avion, and all the other workingman's pubs. The King Edward, the Queen's, and their ilk will survive, somehow. But not the Shamrock, I am certain. Not the Nipissing.

The Guinness, dark and smooth, disappears, and I order another. With a second Union Label, I sit back, drink, smoke, stare through the blue air, letting the odors penetrate, cling to me, avoiding going home.

I have no plan.

The place fills up, the noise grows, and I sink gratefully into the haze, let the hours slip by.

At eight o'clock I give the waiter a ten-dollar bill, accept a five back, wave off the change, and find myself standing on the street outside, collar turned up against the cold. I walk south on River to Queen, then west through Irish Cabbagetown.

Sumach Street, then Sackville.

At Sackville, I pause. This is where my sister Bridget and her husband Charles and their four children live. Bridget, I think. Only four years older than me, whom I seldom see anymore. Like Rose, only two years my senior, now with Neil and their three on Sherbourne Street, which I will pass in a half-dozen blocks or so. Rose: the Nipissing comes back to me, odors, textures, as does a sudden flash of even earlier images: Kate, Teresa, Bridget, Rose, and I crossing the Grand River on our way to St. Mary's School. Miss Lecour. Bridget, Rose, and I, huddled beneath heavy blankets in the same room: the sound of their breathing, of Rose coughing.

Maybe it is the Guinness, the blarney about St. Patrick that floated through the pub, but I begin to think, as I note the faces on the street about me, that perhaps I belong here. I think of Peter Sterling, an Englishman, who employed me, paid me for eighteen years, yet never knew me, never wanted to know me. Who let me go. Who let us all go.

I walk on.

At Power Street, I stop: another memory.

Lillian. Eighteen years ago. The hayloft at Boyd's farm, the woods beside the Don River.

I turn down the street, stop outside Osgoode Dairy, number 82, wonder about Lillian, her mother, her three brothers, if they are still there, atop it. Then I see different people moving about through the windows, in the gaslight, and I know that they are not, that they are gone, like so much else. Eighteen years ago.

At my back is St. Paul's Roman Catholic Church. I cross over, push through the creaking wooden doors, slide into a richly lacquered pew near the back. It is warmer inside, and there is the church smell, the incense. At the front, over the altar, is a painting of the Last Supper; above that, in the domed recess, is a large mural of a man dying, whom I take to be St. Paul, amid warriors, angels, and rays that part the clouds. Between the two paintings I read the Latin inscription *Saule Saule Quid Me Persequeris?* which I do not understand. I count nine more paintings, from front to back, adorning the ceiling, high overhead. I glance about at the three-dimensional carvings that are the stations of the cross, at the cloth-draped confessionals—remember kneeling in ones just like them as a boy.

I do not know how I came here. I do not attend church. Margaret was baptized in St. Cecilia's, Jack in St. Helen's. Soon there will be Margaret's first communion. Places for rituals only, I think, where we are assigned roles. Nothing more.

Yet sitting here, in shadow, I am drawn to the flickering tiers of votive candles behind colored glass, red, green, the possibility of contact, of help. I rise, walk to the side altar, light a candle, drop a nickel into the brass box, watch the wax begin to flow, to settle. I think of Kervin, Mike, Ma, of John and Bill, boys, covered in mud, clutching rifles somewhere in Europe, of Gramma in a blue nightgown, propped against a white pillow. I think of my father, a blacksmith, leaving Elora, leaving his trade, living and dying in a city he did not know, that did not know him, thousands of miles from his birthplace, and folding my hands I stand there and say what I hope is a prayer.

I am on the sidewalk outside Don Valley Pressed Bricks, staring at the stone facade of the building. I think, again, about eighteen years. Then I walk to Berna Motors and Taxicabs at Victoria and Adelaide, flop into the backseat of a cab, light another cigar, and tell the driver to take me home, take me to Lansdowne Avenue, to Maggie, Margaret, Jack. When we arrive, I pay the driver two dollars, tell him to keep the change, stumble inside, up the stairs.

The door opens easily. Maggie is waiting for me, fear in her eyes. I go to her, hold her hands, drop my head, shamed. The children are quiet, watching, listening.

She looks at me.

I shrug my shoulders. I know I smell badly, of beer, cigars.

Then I realize: I am doing it again. This, I think, is how I first came to her, those many years ago, in Simpson's, my hat lying on the counter between us.

I am tired, cold. I am about to disappoint people again. But before I do, before their faces turn from me, I take the envelope out of my pocket, with my letter, with forty-three dollars left, and hand it to Maggie, my offering, all that I have.

2

151 McDougall Ave.
Detroit, Mich.
May 7, 1916

410 Lansdowne Ave.
Toronto, Ont.

Dear Martin,

Got your letter last week with the news of Kervin's death and your being let go at work. Things don't sound too good but don't despair as things always pick up. Please give Cora and my sympathy to everyone. Cora is worried about her own brother (Morris) because he has enlisted in the army and it just seems like a matter of time before the Yanks too will be going abroad for this bloody war so these things visit us all.

I have some news of my own. Cora is now pregnant and we are expecting the baby in November. But here's the other news, by November we'll be back in Toronto as Ford is opening a plant there at the corner of Dupont and Christie and I applied for a promotion there and got it! I start in September. It didn't hurt any that I was born and raised in the city and knew important people like you! I'll sure miss some of the folks at the plant, like Walter as we go back a long way, and Cora and his wife Mary Alice have become quite *good friends. There's something about going home though that I find irresistible and Cora remembers her trip to your wedding so fondly that she didn't take much convincing. The only one she is close to in her family is her brother Morris and I already told you about him.*

Say, are you interested in seeing if you can get on at the plant too? I can look into it if you'd like, just let me know.

> *Tootin my horn,*
> *Jock*

> *410 Lansdowne Ave.*
> *Toronto, Ont.*
> *June 11, 1916*

151 McDougall Ave.
Detroit, Mich.

Dear Jock,

Great news on both counts—that you will be a daddy and that you and Cora will be coming to Toronto. Congratulations twice! (And a promotion, what a big shot.) I look forward to getting together again often.

My news is that I've got a new job. I'm working in the Receiving Department on the 7th floor of Simpson's. Yes Simpson's. Maggie worked at Simpson's, as you know, and Mike has always worked for them, so they found out about the opening and put in the word for me. If they hadn't done so, I trust that I might be working for you underneath a flivver at Dupont and Christie pretty soon. By the way—they are selling Model Ts here for $360 now. Can you believe it? But my chances of ever getting one are still slim and none. Oh well.

But the real sad news is that you cannot get a beer anywhere decent. There are bootleggers everywhere, but the bottled stuff that's been hoarded is worth a king's ransom. It's the story of my life that I didn't even think about putting away my own stash the way so many others did. The rumor is that it's just a matter of time before the temperance ladies get organized south of the border and it hits you there too, especially if your boys all leave for the fighting in Europe, so tell Cora to have her family stock up. It could be the door to a wonderful opportunity.

See you in September, old man. And as for the blessing of the baby, get ready to never sleep in again. And remember, the only way we'll get to have a beer together is if you bring lots with you, and pack it so deep under your belongings that the customs boys will collapse of exhaustion and boredom rather than keep digging.

> *Yours, with a dry throat,*
> *Martin*

3

GRAMMA HAS A TERRIBLE COUGH, HARSH, A FEEBLE BARK. HER nose is running. She is pale, her hair uncombed. Today, she does not drink the tea I offer her in the thermos lid, has no interest in it. Her head sinks into the white pillow, her mouth open, her eyes glazed. Unmoving, her hands lie like bleached driftwood at her sides, palms down. The bottle of Lourdes water sits on the bedside table.

It is February 4, 1917, and the cold of winter seeps beneath every baseboard, pours silently through the panes of every window, penetrates to the bone. It is impossible to be warm, even with the coals glowing in the stove nearby.

I touch the skin on the back of her hand, as cold as the room, and wonder again how old she is. Eighty-five? Ninety? And then I wonder about a life that stopped in 1845, that has atrophied in shock ever since, letting the world swirl around it.

She coughs, sudden, hoarse, rasping, gasps air back into liquid lungs, and I know, without knowing how, that I am fortunate to be here with her now, at this moment, in this brittle room, where there are only the two of us.

"Margaret," I say. "Margaret Loy."

The eyes, milky, perhaps blind, turn to me. Her lips are cracked, dry.

"It's me. Martin. I'm here." Then I say it the old way: "Mártain." I hold her hand. "I am fine."

Then her mouth makes the *o*, feebly, one last time, and I smile while I feel her fingers tighten on mine as I hoped they would, as she hears her husband's name, her son's name. As I try to give her this.

The priest comes later that afternoon and anoints her with the holy oils, as he has done so many times before. After death is better than not at all, he tells us, bending to his task, to the administration of the sacrament: her eyes, her mouth, her ears, her hands. He weaves the rosary beads through her still, thin fingers as he talks: I am not too late, he says. God will accept her.

I look at Ma. Her face is a mask, pulled tight. I put my arm around her shoulder, feel her go rigid, think to myself what I have often thought since that first time I helped her with Gramma, helped Ma lift her back into her bed, that I am touching her, that I want to touch her before she too is gone.

Twelve

January 1920

RADEY—At her late residence, 38 Brookfield Street, on January 19, 1920, Ann, widow of the late John Radey, in her 75th year.

Funeral Wednesday at 8:30 A.M., to St. Francis Church. Interment St. Michael's Cemetery.

The Toronto Daily Star
Tuesday, January 20, 1920

The priest takes the crucifix from the top of the casket and hands it to Mary, who, white faced, clutches it in both hands. Elizabeth and Kate are holding one another, crying.

Ma is lowered into the ground. With Da. It seems impossible. They are still alive in my head, always. I will talk to them forever. The sky is gray, the wind biting. The two of them, I think. Born across the ocean and buried so far away, in this frozen, snowy ground, sixteen seeds scattered.

I will be forty in June. At the grave's edge, my parents in the earth, I now understand what it means to be the youngest in a family of older parents: I will experience all the death around me sooner than my siblings did, everyone will likely go before me, this will happen to me more often than it will to the others, this standing at a grave's edge. I am in a different place. My life will be different.

And I am an orphan.

My brother, my sisters. We are all orphans.

Loy, I think, is the Irish for shovel.

A flock of starlings rises up against the bleak winter sky, heads east.

We are back at Mary's, at number 38. The women are in the kitchen. They are slicing egg salad sandwiches, tuna sandwiches, baloney sandwiches, tomato and mayonnaise sandwiches, all into small triangles, arranging them on plates. The men are in the living room smoking cigarettes, cigars, drinking coffee, tea, or beer, which has been supplied mysteriously by my friend Jock, who is here. Margaret and the older children are with the youngest ones in the bedrooms upstairs, keeping them quiet. Erector sets, snakes and ladders, checkers, the Street Car game. Maggie has given them a copy of both *The American Boys Handy Book* and *The American Girls Handy Book*, and when all else fails they will use them for instructions to tie knots of every kind, make a boomerang, fold a daisy fan from paper, make an armed war kite.

Jock, Mike, John Manion, John Dickinson, Neil Kernaghan, Oliver Johnson, and I sip Jock's beer and discuss the prohibition laws, which were passed only last week in the United States, making the entire country as dry as we've been here in Ontario for four years now. We tell Jock that he is our savior, offer a toast to him, listen to his tale of buying Pabst Near Beer and mixing it with alcoholic malt tonic from

the drugstore, and, chuckling, shake our heads in amazement
that we didn't think of it.

Jim Bedford, Peter Curtis, Michael Rossiter, Jim McKenna,
Charles Trader—all tell us it is too early, that they cannot
face a drink before noon, and we wonder what is wrong with
them, tease them.

We are all here, as we should be, and I think that Ma
would be pleased.

*Personal items found in Ann Radey's bedroom
after her death*

white chamoisette gloves—boxed, never worn
pair of eyeglasses
photo of Martin and Mike—"April 7, 1886, Elora,"
    printed on back
ten 4½" shell hairpins
pincushion with hat pins
pompadour comb
statue of St. Anthony
rosary
packet of letters
death certificates for Sarah Radey O' Brien 1885,
    baby boy Radey 1870, Patrick Francis Radey 1884,
    Loretta Radey 1885, Margaret Loy Whalen 1917,
    John Radey 1906
baptismal certificates for Sarah, Julia, Margaret, Mike,
    Mary, Ann, Elizabeth, Kate, Bridget, Rose, Emma,
    Teresa, Patrick, Martin, Loretta
locket with photo of Sarah Radey inside
$5 American gold piece
Beecham's pills
box of Peps for winter coughs

bottle of Bayer aspirin
cherrywood jewelry box
Cuticura soap
pair of wooden shoe inserts
metal shoehorn
box of buttons
nail clippers
crucifix
dried palm fronds
bottle of Lourdes water

Maggie and Margaret and Jack and I move, to an apartment at 1505 Dundas West, which we hope will give us all more space. The children are getting older and need their own rooms.

Thirteen

October 6, 1923

1

SUNNYSIDE BEACH
Toronto's Lakeside Playground
Publicly Owned and Controlled

130 Acres of Pleasure
2 Miles of Boulevards and Promenade
Amusement Devices, Games, Rides, Beach Chairs, and
Refreshments
Boating, Canoeing and Dancing
Band Concerts Every Evening

BATHING PAVILION
7,700 Individual Lockers. Sterilized Suits and Towels.
Hot and Cold Showers. Diving Platforms and Water Slides.
Safety Floats. Water and Beach Flood-Lighted.
First-Aid Room in Charge of Graduate Nurse.
Hair-Drying, Hair-Dressing, and Manicuring.

Professional Swimming Instructors.
Life-Guards in Charge of Beach.
Terrace Gardens, Refreshments and Orchestra.

TWENTY MINUTES BY STREET CAR, FIFTEEN MINUTES BY MOTOR FROM DOWN-TOWN.

At 10 A.M. on Saturday, October 6, 1923, I alight from the streetcar at the Queen-King-Roncesvalles-Lake Shore intersection with Jack who is twelve, Margaret, fourteen, accompanied by Jock and his almost seven-year-old daughter, Gail. It is sunny, cool, bright, temperature in the sixties, one of the last nice days we will see before the weather turns, and I pull the brim of my boater low to shade my eyes from the glare. As we pass Tamblyn Drug Store, Jock ducks inside, emerging a few minutes later with a smug grin which he does not explain. Taking his cue, I pop into the United Cigar Store for three Havana Eden Perfectos which I slip into my jacket pocket for later.

Surrounding us are the billboards: Coca-Cola, Old Chum Tobacco, Sunnyside Hair Dressing Parlor, Laura Secord candies, Cozens Spring Service, Columbia Six, Autolene Motor Oils, Neilson chocolates, Players Navy Cut Cigarettes, Boulevard Garage and $1 Taxi. In the distance, on the hill, is the Sunnyside Orphanage, a strange juxtaposition to this place of childish diversions. In the opposite direction, on another rise, I can see the tiled roof and sign of the Sunnyside railway station. Tomorrow, bright and early, Jack and Margaret and I will board the new CNR line there for the forty-mile trip to Hamilton to see Maggie.

We step carefully across the maze of intersecting streetcar tracks, complicated beyond belief, descend the steep stairway to the amusement park, and I listen to Gail as she squeals with delight, cannot wait any longer, and pulls on Jock's arm.

* * * *

The Flyer roller coaster dominates against the sky, its trolley of cars with screaming passengers rising and falling rhythmically every few minutes, a clock's pendulum. The crowds are here already. Lineups for the Dutch Mill, the golf putting course, Fun Land, Pick Your Car.

Jock puts Gail on the merry-go-round, stands at its rim as she circles. Both their faces, I see, are glowing. Jack and Margaret scurry off to try the Frolic and the Dodgem. When they return, I give them some more money for games: the Monkey Racer, the fish pond, the Kentucky Derby, and they take Gail with them, holding her hands on either side, and I am proud as I watch them.

The Aero Swing seems tame enough for Gail so we say to Jack and Margaret, all right, fine, you can take her with you, and I light one of my three Havanas while I stand and watch the three of them. Jock is poking about inside his shoulder bag, which he has set down on a wooden picnic table, busy at something. I can't help but focus on Jack and Margaret, my two, glorious in what little remains of their childhood, as they lift upward, then swoop down, again and again, heads thrown back, white teeth flashing.

We eat red hots, french fries in a vortex cup, choose among Honey Dew, Hires Rootbeer, Vernor's ginger ale, Frost Kist drinks. At midafternoon there is a giant corn roast taking place on the beach. We give the children some nickels, and while Margaret and Jack take Gail to watch Tiny Tim, the dancing bear who has made an appearance there, Jock reaches into his shoulder bag and takes out two thermos bottles, hands me one, winks, and we settle back on a bench, the children visible in the distance.

"You sly dog, you." I watch Jock unscrew the top of his thermos, pour the foamy, cool brew into the lid.

"Pabst—mixed with alcoholic malt tonic as usual, direct from Sunnyside's own Tamblyn's."

I take out the two remaining Havanas, offer Jock one, and we light up, sipping our brew, kings.

The children are lined up for ears of roasted corn, patient. Tiny Tim rivets everyone on the beach.

"You seen the brick of wine you can buy?" asks Jock.

I shake my head. "Don't know what you're talking about."

"New York state vintner is selling a solid block of grape concentrate, about the size of a pound of butter. It comes with instructions that warn that if you add water, you'll have wine, and that would be illegal." He smiles. "Fella at work showed it to me."

I snort. "That's what gave Harding the heart attack. The hypocrisy. That and the fact that all his cronies were dipping into the public till. His attorney general somehow managed to bank seventy-five thousand dollars on a salary of twelve thousand dollars a year." I send a stream of blue smoke into the air. "Mackenzie King and Coolidge. Prime minister, president, doesn't matter. They got their heads in the sand too. They say Coolidge spends from two to four hours every working day taking a nap."

Jock chuckles. "And the rest of the time he gets driven around in a Pierce-Arrow, waiting for problems to solve themselves."

"I'd like to have a nap every day."

"Isn't that what you do up there on the seventh floor?"

"And then I'd like to have a tall, cool beer and a nice supper, every night, put my feet up."

We are quiet, watching the children, the dancing bear, content.

Jock seems to know what I am thinking. "How is Maggie doing?"

I shrug. "She needed the break, the rest. The kids are looking forward to seeing her tomorrow." I add: "So am I."

"You haven't talked about it much."

I cannot talk about it, I think. Men do not talk about things they do not understand, as women seem to do, turning situations and people over verbally, parsing them, tasting them, telling each other what someone not present thinks.

"I haven't seen you enough. Busy. Families keep you busy."

"Amen." He drinks, squints into the sun.

"The fainting spells have been going on for too long. Heart palpitations. No one's sure why. Pale, no energy."

"And this doctor she's seeing?"

"In Hamilton. He's supposed to be a specialist at this sort of thing, so her sister Nellie arranged for her to stay with friends of hers there for the week. The Wilsons. They're putting her up, no charge. Very kind. We can't afford any of it as it is."

Jock listens.

"What can you do?" I ask.

He is quiet for a while. We smoke our Havanas. Then he points to the beach, to Jack and Margaret and Gail. "Watch the dancing bear," he says.

When the children come back, it is Jack who looks at the thermos, smells it, and I note the small cloud of disapproval rise behind his eyes—so like his mother—a cumulus that I have seen floating there more and more frequently. It is becoming clearer. It has always been Jack who judges me, whom I cannot win over fully, who puzzles me, and I wonder, again, what it is I am doing wrong.

2

WHEN JACK AND MARGARET ARE FINALLY ASLEEP, I SIT IN THE maroon upholstered easy chair, feet up, enjoying reading the newspaper by electric light. One of the attractions of this Berkeley Street flat is that it is electrically wired, the first that we have lived in. At forty-three, though, I cannot read without eyeglasses, which bothers me, because even they do not stop the strain, fatigue, and I dab at my eyes with my handkerchief, rub them often. Still, the light is a wonder, a marvel.

There is a wooden mantle over the stove, and beside the earphones to the crystal set I see the mix of books lined up atop it: *Seventeen, The U.P. Trail, Mr. Britling Sees It Through, Penrod, Tarzan of the Apes, Tom Swift and His Motor-Cycle, This Side of Paradise, Main Street, The Scarlet Letter, The Shoes of Happiness* by Edwin Markham, whom Maggie tells me is her favorite poet, others.

I have no favorite poet. Only one of the books is mine, one of the two copies of *Sister Carrie* that is also there.

I take my eyeglasses off, hold them by the spidery wire rims in my hands, polish the lenses with my handkerchief. We must be up early tomorrow. Forty miles is a long trip.

I dream again that night of Jack slipping off the wooden dock into the lake, beneath the surface. He does not come up. I dive into the black water, stay under for ages, lungs burning, cannot find him. Oh God, please God.

He is gone.

I wake up sweating, only Maggie is not here. I am alone. No one strokes my head, my brow.

As always, I am cold.

I stare into the darkness, calming myself.

Fourteen

I sit in darkness. I sit in human silence. Then I begin to hear the eloquent night, the night of wet trees, with moonlight sliding over the shoulder of the church in a haze of dampness and subsiding heat.

—THOMAS MERTON
The Sign of Jonas

I WAS NOT SURE WHERE WE WERE, BUT THE FLOCK SEEMED higher than usual, the earth below more rounded, the vista more sweeping. A waving necklace of honking geese undulated in the distance, a flat ribbon of silver river coiling beneath us in the sun.

Time and space and memory unrolled into one giant net and we, black birds against the blue sky, slipped through larger holes and back through others. I imagined that I spoke to my grandmother, silent still, even now, explaining what I was seeing, what I was experiencing, wanting her to know, wondered if she was listening, knew that she was listening, inside me, outside me, somewhere, somehow, knew that she had not died, not really, because I could see her so clearly, and understood now that family is a memory that transcends words.

Time happened to the world below, froze there, forever, everything, and memory was needed to make time happen to my mind. And in my mind I heard women's voices, so many women, muffling the sharp silence of men who could not speak, who felt but could not share, could not touch. Alone.

My own family, small, lost in the numbers, in the crush of time, insignificant. Except to me. Except to me.

High, in the wind. Mother, Father. Talk to me. Oh, Maggie.

Fifteen

January–May 1926

1

It is 8:30 p.m., Wednesday, January 6, 1926. We are in the kitchen at 10 Constance Street in the west end, near Bloor and Roncesvalles, our new flat of only two weeks.

Our first day here was the day before Christmas and Margaret and Jack got to celebrate by waking up to parcels under the tree. Mike, my brother, a widower with half his family grown and gone, now lives in a small place out on Queen East—on Lockwood Road—with his son Carmen, eighteen, and his two grown daughters, Ann and Kathleen. Mike has left Simpson's. For the past two years he has worked for the gas company, and has managed to get Carmen hired on with him. Still enamored of his wagon though, ever reliable, it was he who helped us drag our worldly possessions across the city.

Now that I am making twenty-four dollars a week, we are moving up in the world. The new flat costs thirty dollars a month. It has four bright rooms, a bath, water heating and oak floors, a telephone. There are rosebushes that will bloom in the spring and summer, a verandah. Maggie likes it because she feels that she is closer to her roots and to the Junction. Margaret, attending St. Joseph's Convent School, and Jack at De La Salle, both find it more convenient too.

At one end of the kitchen table Margaret finishes listing out her Latin verbs, conjugating each into its four parts. Jack is reading the comics from *The Toronto Star: Bringing Up Father, Gasoline Alley, Tillie the Toiler, Polly and Her Pals, Toots and Casper, Winnie Winkle—The Breadwinner.*

Margaret takes a card out of her notebook as she closes it, handing it to me. "I got this Monday from Sister Josephine," she says. It is a picture of the sacred heart of Jesus. On the back is the inscription *To Margaret Radey, January 4, 1926, for fifth place on the honor roll.*

I look at her. She is a marvel. Yet her innocence unsettles me. She seems so easily pleased, so naturally happy.

Margaret, her mind elsewhere, changes the topic. "Did the new radios arrive at Simpson's?"

Even Jack looks up now, interested.

It was Monday at dinner, I recall, that I mentioned the shipment that we were expecting. "We got fifty of them. They came in today."

"When can we get one?" Jack asks.

I frown through my eyeglasses and cigar smoke. It would be nice, I think. Kate and Jim have a radio. Mike and Liz talked about getting one even back at the end of the war. But, I think, they waited too long.

It could be playing right now. We could all be listening to it. "Ain't We Got Fun," "I'm Sitting on Top of the World," "When You're Smiling."

"What kind are they?" Jack persists.

"Atwater-Kent," I say.

Jack listens intently. I notice Margaret and Maggie paying

attention too. "Five-tube sets. One seventy-nine fifty. That's a lot of money," I add.

Their eyes waver. They know the phrase. *That's a lot of money.*

But we gave ourselves a washing machine as a Christmas present, and it cost $120. Few have $120; but most, including us, can find fifteen dollars down and five dollars a month. The fact that the machine cannot equal the dirt-removing ability of the washboard and scrub brush and old-fashioned elbow grease, or that Maggie often calls on me to disentangle clothes from the sprockets, has not lessened our fascination with it. It is a marvel, and affordable. Payments are the key. Jock has bought a General Electric refrigerator on payments. Everything is available on payments.

The children wait. Even Maggie is smiling, knowing.

I have always wanted to give them everything, without having anything. I smile. Nothing is new. I am forty-five years old, living in rented rooms. I still have nothing, but I can afford the payment. Everybody makes payments nowadays. A radio, I think. Why not. I know the terms. Twenty dollars down, fifteen dollars a month. After all, I am making twenty-eight dollars a week. These are prosperous times. And there is the employee discount.

I think again of Mike, who waited too long. I think of all the things we have done without. I look at the three of them. Jack, especially, waits. This would be something for all of us. I say it aloud. "Why not?"

"Oh, Martin," says Maggie.

"Like the washing machine," I say.

Jack stands up, excited. Margaret smiles the smile that melts me.

Suddenly I am feeling magnanimous. Things are changing for the better. I can feel it. "This Saturday," I say. "We can all go together to get one, make a day of it." The idea grows, takes on its own life. I see a picture of us in my head as a family, doing something together. "We'll go in the morning, and then we'll have lunch at the Palm Room on the sixth floor. The chicken dinner is on special this week for a dollar." I have seen the signs in the cafeteria downstairs. "There's an orchestra."

Margaret gets up, surprises me by hugging me. Even Jack, his expression always wry, is nodding rare approval.

I look to Maggie, who even though pale, never fully well, is smiling. "There'll be giblet gravy, rhubarb pie," I say, waiting for her approval.

"Oh, Martin," she says, giving it, smiling. Knowing me.

2

IT IS A DREAM, A BAD DREAM, BEYOND IMAGINING.

I am out of body as I crouch down beside her where she has slumped on the bathroom floor. I must be somewhere else, I think, as I hear myself shouting her name.

Margaret is beside me, her hands covering her mouth, her eyes wide. Jack is standing in the doorway, face frozen in shock. The tap is still running.

Even squeezing her, holding her, I cannot make her talk to me. Maggie! I shout. What happened? What happened? Her skin beneath my fingers is white, like chalk.

She just fell, says Margaret. Call your father, she said. And she fell. She was washing my face.

Jack! I shout. Go downstairs. Tell Mrs. Birnbaum I need help. Tell her quick. Hurry!

I loosen her collar, shout her name again, again, try breathing into her mouth, shout her name again. Come back I think. Not now, not now or ever, oh, God, no, please, no.

My mouth is on hers, her lips cold. No, I think. No.

My eyes blur with water, I cannot see. I cannot think.

Margaret is crying. I am crying. I am holding her now, squeezing her, desperate. Maggie, oh Maggie.

And in my head I hear her say it as I clutch her, although her lips, that curl downward at the corners, even now, especially now, do not move, will never move again. *Oh, Martin.*

I'd say it was myocardial failure, a Dr. Harcourt tells me, using words I have never heard before. How old was she? he asks.

Forty-seven, I hear myself say. She would have been forty-eight in three weeks. On January 29.

It just happens, he says. Nothing could be done.

I look around me, at the faces of Margaret, Jack, Mrs. Birnbaum.

I don't know what he means, nothing could be done. I don't know what he means.

What should I do? I ask.

You'll need to call a funeral home, he says.

Margaret and Jack are both crying.

I don't know a funeral home, I say, scarcely believing that I am saying it.

He nods, takes a pen and piece of paper from his bag, writes on it. Here, he says. Lynett's, on Dundas. They'll take care of everything.

I look at him, at the piece of paper, make no move to take it. I cannot talk. He realizes this, folds it, puts it in his pocket. I'll call them he says. Do you have a phone?

Mrs. Birnbaum is crying too now.

Yes, I say. Yes. We have a phone.

I cannot just let them take her. It isn't right. I go with them without knowing why, since there is nothing that I can do.

We sit in a room on opposite sides of a large desk and I am asked questions while forms are completed and I sign them. They are good enough to bring me home, and after I come home, in the middle of the night, my hands shaking, dizzy, I sit on the bed between Margaret and Jack, my arms around them, and we cry, all of us, finally, for as long as it takes.

RADEY—Suddenly on January 6, at her late residence, 10 Constance Street, Margaret (Maggie) Curtis, dearly beloved wife of Martin J. Radey.

Funeral from above address Saturday 9th at 8:45 A.M. to St. Vincent de Paul Church. Interment in Peacemount Cemetery, Dixie, Ont.

The Toronto Daily Star
Thursday, January 7, 1926

MR. MARTIN RADEY and FAMILY
acknowledge with grateful appreciation
your kind expression of sympathy
in their bereavement

10 Constance Street
Toronto

On March 1, we leave 10 Constance Street. We cannot stay here. It will never be the same. Jack, Margaret, and I, with Mike's help, move to a flat on Margueretta Street. It is not as nice or as big, but it does not matter.

My brother and I have always been close, but now the bond runs deeper. First his wife, Liz, then Maggie. Even so, something is bothering him. He is not himself. He tells me that his mouth is sore, that he thinks there might be something wrong with his teeth. He worries about gum disease, which Da always talked about, but neither of us know exactly what it is, so we drop the subject. He says that if Liz were here, she would know what the problem was, know the right medicine.

I go to work daily. Margaret and Jack go to school. On the sixteenth of the month, I pay the woman at the accounts wicket in Simpson's five dollars for the washing machine. Nobody mentions the radio again.

On Tuesday, April 6, before I can even get my coat off, Jack comes to me when I come in the door after work. "Father?"

I take off my hat, place it on the table. "What is it?"

"My arm hurts."

"Where?" I ask, trying not to seem annoyed. I am tired. Patience, I think. Patience.

He touches his right forearm with his left hand. "Here," he says. "It hurts here."

"What did you do to it?"

"I fell."

"Where?" I ask. "When? How?" Jack tells me nothing voluntarily. I must ask for everything.

"On the way to school. I was leaping from a fence, grabbing onto a tree branch, swinging. I fell. I landed on the sidewalk. It's been hurting ever since."

"That sounds like a stupid thing to do."

He says nothing.

"You went to school though?"

"Yes."

"It can't be too bad then."

He drops his eyes.

I watch his face. He is in a pain of some kind. "Let me see it," I say.

Gently, he lifts it, holds it out. I take it carefully, unbutton the cuff, roll up the sleeve. There is some swelling. I touch it.

Jack winces, tries not to pull away.

I do not know what to do. Maggie would have cradled it, kissed it, held him, stroked his hair, soothed his woe. I know this. I have seen her do it.

But I cannot do it. I have never done it.

"Can you move your fingers?"

He wiggles them.

"There. It can't be too bad then, can it?"

I look closely at his face. It is streaked with dirt. It is possible that he has been crying. He looks up at me.

Margaret comes into the room, stands, watches.

I meet her eyes. She smiles.

"Jack hurt his arm," she says.

"Yes. He told me." I let his arm drop, put my hand on his shoulder. "You'll be all right. It's just a bruise. Go and wash up. Your face and hands." I glance at Margaret. "How's dinner coming?"

"Baked potatoes and sausages. It's almost ready."

"Good." I take off my jacket, hang it on the wall hook, unfold the newspaper I have been carrying, eye my reading chair.

Jack is still looking at me.

"Jack."

"Yes sir." He turns and leaves, heading for the bathroom. Margaret goes back into the kitchen.

I stand alone, watching them disappear.

The next evening for dinner Margaret cooks bacon and boiled potatoes. I watch Jack favoring his right arm as he eats. We have plums for dessert.

"How's your arm?"

"Sore." He does not meet my eyes.

I am quiet, thinking, wondering what to do. Wondering what Maggie would do.

Jack is eating his plums with his left hand.

"Maybe we should soak it in warm water after dinner. What do you think?"

He looks up.

"We could do it in the sink," says Margaret. "I'll help."

I am grateful for her offer.

"Would you like that, Jack?"

He shrugs. "Yes," he says.

After dinner, I fill the sink with warm water, but I step aside and let Margaret handle the bathing. Her touch is soft, gentle, feminine. Exactly what Jack needs, I think. Exactly what I need.

On Thursday I smell the bacon and fried potatoes Margaret is cooking for dinner when I come in the door.

"Where's Jack?" I ask as I head for my reading chair.

"In his room."

Before I can ask how he is, Margaret approaches me.

"He's in his room. He's been crying."

I look up at her from my chair, surprised.

"He came home from school early."

After a day at work, I have to orient myself to their world, try to remember what has been happening in his life that may have caused this, but can come up with nothing.

"I think there's something badly wrong with his arm, Father. He was sent home because he couldn't write with it today. He hasn't been writing anything at all for three days. He's been pretending in classes, but his English teacher finally discovered what he'd been up to when he asked him to write on the board and he couldn't."

I get up from my chair, go to Jack's room, open the door. He is lying on his back on the bed with his eyes closed, His right arm is across his chest. There is a sheen of sweat on his brow. His mouth is open.

At St. Michael's Hospital, they place the arm in a cast. Broken, they tell me. The forearm. We had to break it again to set it. Should have had him in here right away, they tell me. Three days? Why so long?

He didn't tell me, I say.

They look at me quietly.

Did he tell his mother?

She's dead, I tell them.

They are quiet.

I didn't know what to do. I didn't understand.

More silence.

I didn't know what to do.

They say no more.

At dinner on Monday, Jack shows Margaret the signatures of his classmates that adorn his cast. She signs it and he smiles. Then they laugh.

I do not know if I am supposed to sign it or not, but neither of them ask me, so I content myself with smiling. But I know they would have asked Maggie. They would have. And she would have laughed and written something witty. I know it.

My brother, Mike, at age sixty, is diagnosed with cancer of the jaw. He spends two days in St. Michael's Hospital while they do tests, see how bad it is, whether it can be cut out.

When I go to see him, he is scared, but does not cry, although you can see that he is holding back, that it is what he will probably do as soon as I leave. Carcinoma, he tells me. Carcinoma, they call it.

A month goes by. The carcinoma gets worse, spreads slowly, a laborer toiling for daily wages.

Sixteen

June–August 1926

1

I CANNOT BELIEVE WHAT IS HAPPENING TO MIKE. I HAVE NEVER seen anything like this. It is eating away his jaw, his mouth, his face, and he just sits there and looks at me when I visit—can barely talk. He could not afford to stay in the hospital and since there was little they could do for him there at any rate, he has returned home where all he does is lie in his bed. The doctors fear the worst: that secondary cancers will occur in the neck glands.

When they can afford it, his children, Kathleen, Ann, and Carmen, buy a supply of steaks, and Mike keeps them on his face so that the cancer will eat them instead of him.

Lockwood Avenue is at the other end of the city. I have to take the streetcar out to the east end, then back across the city to where we live in the west end, a distance of about ten miles. Simpson's is midway between the two, so a trip after work becomes more like fifteen miles, and I cannot get home until nine or ten o'clock at night.

Margaret is a gem. She says that she understands, and I think that she does. She has assumed the role of housekeeper and family cook. I would be lost without her. Jack resents my absence. I can see it in his eyes. He misses his mother in a way that makes me feel responsible, and he seldom talks to me.

"I don't feel well, Father." Jack lies in bed instead of rising for school. It is almost June. The cast is off his arm. I am on the verge of ignoring his complaint as a childish attempt to stay home from school, but I remember dismissing his sore arm and am careful.

"What's the matter?"

"I feel sick to my stomach."

I feel his brow, which seems warm. Perhaps he has a fever. I am not sure. I do not even know if we have a thermometer.

"Might be the flu." The flu is nothing to toy with. It killed millions at the end of the war. Everybody knows this.

"Stay in bed," I say suddenly. "Maybe Margaret can stay home with you."

"She has a French test today. She studied for it all last evening." Jack looks at me, eyes widened, glistening.

I did not know this. I did not get home until past ten last night. Dinner was in the oven, Jack and Margaret in bed.

I touch his brow again. "You're fourteen years old," I say. "Can you take care of yourself if I leave you alone today?"

"I'm—" Then he stops, does not finish. His eyes glaze. He nods. His hair is stuck to his scalp with sweat.

"I'll ask Margaret to come straight home from school." I pause. "I'll come straight home too tonight."

He looks at me, hopeful.

"All right?"

"Yes."

"You'll manage?"

He nods again.

"Is there something you can eat?"

"I can make a sandwich."

"Good boy."

Like his mother, I think. Sickly. I've never really noticed if he has always been this sickly.

I am afraid. There is illness everywhere, yet somehow I escape it.

But something else gnaws at me as I leave the house that morning. Jack started to say something, stopped. There was a quiet withdrawal in his eyes. Then it hits me: Jack is not fourteen. He is fifteen. I have forgotten his birthday. April 30. His arm was still in the cast. No one reminded me.

Maggie would have remembered.

I think of my father, coming home past nine o'clock, exhausted, covered in mud and cement, not knowing it was my birthday, ever. I think of the straight-edged razor that was my great-grandfather's, how my father never knew that I had it, how it was my mother who saw to it that these things were passed on, that the little things were remembered and dealt with.

Only now they don't seem so little anymore. Now I am mother and father.

They are huge. They are swallowing me.

That evening Jack throws up in his bed, again and again, before he can get to the bathroom.

I run the water into the bathtub so that he can clean himself, make it cool so that it will fight the fever. At his age I am unsure if I should help him bathe, cool him down. But I cannot bring myself to do it. I close the door on him and leave him alone in the bathroom.

Margaret and I do not finish washing the bedding and cleaning the mattress until past ten, but the sheets are still not dry so we flip the mattress over. Jack can sleep on it without sheets, but I do not know where the spare blankets are kept until Margaret shows me.

It is the weekend before Jack is up and about. The fever has passed.

On Saturday afternoon, I give Margaret money for groceries and lie down on the living room sofa. I am asleep when she calls me for dinner.

We are having corned beef and cabbage.

Monday, on my lunch hour, I saunter into the book department of Eaton's for the second time in my life.

"May I help you?" A bespectacled lady, graying hair.

"Do you sell cookbooks?"

"My, yes. Right over here." She leads me down an aisle, scanning shelves. "What did you have in mind?"

"I don't know."

She looks back over her shoulder at this.

"Something basic," I say.

"For your wife? A gift?"

"For my daughter." I pause. "And for myself."

She stops, looks at me, but says nothing.

"Something basic," I repeat.

She takes a blue, clothbound volume from a shelf at shoulder height, hands it to me. "This one's in its third printing. Very popular. The author, Nellie Lyle Pattinson, used to teach domestic science at Central Technical School."

It is heavy. I flip through it. More than four hundred pages.

"There are chapters on meat, fish, fowl, eggs, salads, sauces, foods cooked in deep fat, fruits—"

I see a photograph of a table setting, with the correct placement of cutlery.

"—soups, pastries, desserts . . ." She trails away. Then:

"There's even chapters on diabetic foods and on meal planning."

I am reading a section called "Chicken Leftovers."

"It's quite modern."

"And this is the one you would recommend?"

"Do you—and your daughter—have another cookbook at home already?"

"No."

"Then this is the one I would recommend."

"How much is it?"

"One ninety-five." Pause. "You can't overemphasize the importance of eating right. Good nutrition equals good health."

I think of Jack, his illness.

Then she does a surprising thing. She touches my forearm. "Buy it," she says. And I realize that she knows. I have become transparent.

On Wednesday I fry three chicken legs in a pan, bake three potatoes. Margaret shucks some corn and boils the cobs.

When we eat, the potatoes are too hard, the chicken still pink inside. Margaret pretends everything is fine. Jack is quiet.

The corn is delicious.

On the streetcar Friday evening, heading home, I see Jack standing on the corner of Bloor and Dufferin in a group of boys his age. They are all smoking cigarettes.

Seeing this, I am depressed. I did not know. I do not want him to smoke. He is too young. And where is he getting the money?

When he comes in the house an hour later, I can smell it on him as he passes. How long has it clung to him like this and I haven't noticed? But I do not say anything. I have avoided lighting up my own cigar, confused again as to what I should be doing.

Maggie. Oh, Maggie. Where are you?

I cannot think straight. It is more than the summer heat. I do not want to go home at night, even for the children. Everything seems to be amiss. I cannot imagine my future, alone. I am forty-six years old, and cannot decide if I am still young or if I am suddenly old.

I miss Maggie.

Too many people are dying all about me. I understand Mike's fear. It is real, palpable. God, I wonder, and close my eyes. What else are you going to do to me, to us?

2

MARGARET, WHO WILL BE SEVENTEEN ON AUGUST 21, HAS A girlfriend, Eleanor Nolan, who goes to St. Joseph's with her, whom she met when we lived east of Yonge, at 198 Berkeley in Cabbagetown. Eleanor and her family live up the street at number 222. Margaret is spending a great deal of time at Eleanor's place, and rather than travel all the way back across the city to our place in the west end, she has taken to staying with my sister Rose and her family on Sherbourne Street. And since Jack would rather be with Margaret than with me, he too spends most of his time in the east end, either with Rose or with Bridget on Sackville, or even at Mike's place, chumming with his cousin Carmen.

I am empty inside. I need more than Jack and Margaret. The space, dark and deep, has not always been there. This is new.

I am alone, for the first time ever.

* * * *

She comes up to me after ten o'clock mass at St. Cecilia's on Annette Street, corner of Pacific Avenue, Sunday, August 15—surprises me, as I am alone, standing on the street at the foot of the stairs. Jack and Margaret have been staying with Rose and her family for the last few days.

"Mr. Radey."

"Yes." The sun shines hotly on us. My Homburg, not yet on my head, is in my hands, and I feel the heat on my brow. I squint into the glare.

"I'm Gertrude McNulty." A strong face, confident, determined, peers out from beneath the feathered Sunday hat. Much younger than me, I think.

She extends her hand.

I take it gently—not like I would a man's—still unsure of what I should say, of why she is talking to me. Instead of words, I smile.

"You were pointed out to me," she says.

I tilt my head sideways, still holding her hand.

"I wanted to say how sorry I am for your loss." She hesitates. "I've lost loved ones too."

I am touched. A stranger, I think. I cover the hand I am holding with my left one as well and squeeze it softly. "Thank you. That's very kind of you."

She smiles demurely, pleased.

"I'm surprised that anyone would know enough about me to point me out to anyone. Especially here. I haven't exactly been a regular." I go to churches for funerals now, I think. Then I remember St. Paul's, that night years ago, when I slipped into a back pew, lit a candle, when I sensed things unraveling inside me. When I needed help. And now I am back, trying again. I have nothing to lose.

"Father Colliton told me. I asked him who you were." She drops her eyes. "Forward of me, I know."

I shrug. "My daughter was baptized here." Realizing that

161

I am still holding her hand, I let it slide free, collect my thoughts. "That was a long time ago."

I notice that she is paying attention, listening intently. Then I see her as a woman: dark hair, feminine, attractive, warm, without being pretty, and remember the softness of her hand. A woman's hand. "I've only recently moved back into the area. I've a place on Margueretta Street."

Her eyes, wide set, crinkle in the sun. She nods sharply, a decision made. "Let me buy you a coffee."

"Pardon?"

"There's a place up on Dundas, just up the street, real close. It's open Sundays."

I shuffle my feet, almost embarrassed, glance over my shoulder as if gauging the distance.

"Unofficial welcome back to the parish."

Then I study her more closely. There is intelligence in the eyes, warmth in the smile, honesty in the face. And what am I going to do today anyway? City ordinance laws let us do virtually nothing on Sundays. She has reached out to me, whatever her motives, and I want to accept, want someone to talk to, perhaps more than I know.

"Have you had breakfast?"

"I don't eat much in the morning." I wait until she is seated before sliding into the booth opposite her. The diner is small but clean. I have not been here before.

"Do you cook?"

"Not much," I admit.

She nods, opens the menu in front of her. "You need to eat."

"No, really." I take my hat off, set it on the bench beside me.

"Really," she says.

*   *   *   *

She orders two fresh farm eggs (scrambled) with toast from the menu—an order for both of us—along with two Blue Ribbon coffees.

"That's too much. Too expensive." I am adding it up: thirty plus thirty plus ten plus ten. Eighty cents. "I don't need it."

"Nonsense. I said I'd buy. My treat. Sunday is a day of rest. We've been to church, fed our souls. Now we should treat ourselves, feed our bodies. It's almost noon."

She has not taken her hat off. The eyes that peer out at me are framed by that strong face, her mouth set firm, smiling. She folds her hands on the table in front of her.

"Do you know everybody in the parish?" I ask, accepting.

"Most."

I nod. "And what did Father Colliton tell you about me?"

"That your wife passed away just after Christmas. That you have two teenagers." She pauses. "That you seem quite alone."

I nod again. The coffee is placed on the table in front of us. We tinker with the sugar, the cream, paper napkins, providing breathing space, thinking space. Finally, I lift the cup toward my lips and say, "Thanks for the coffee."

"You're quite welcome."

"And the breakfast."

She smiles broadly.

"What do you do, Mr. Radey?"

"Call me Martin."

"Friends call me Gert." The smile.

"I'm thinking of being a monk," I say, playfully. "I wouldn't have to change much. Clothing, perhaps. I'd get my meals prepared for me. That would solve my cooking problem. Learn to make some wine, some cheese. It's not such a bad deal."

We both smile.

"I'm a receiver at Simpson's."

"Really. That sounds like a good job."

I remember another conversation about jobs, good or otherwise: tea at a corner table, Bowles' Restaurant, Queen and Bay. I clear my head. "I guess," I say. "What about yourself?"

"I'm a telephone operator at Swift's."

"The meat company?"

She nods.

"That's just north of the tracks. Real close. Convenient."

"We're definitely locals."

"Who's we?"

"I live with my mother, who's widowed. And my sister. Just the three of us. On Gilmour Avenue."

"I don't think I know Gilmour."

"It crosses Annette about ten blocks west of here."

"A little farther west than I usually go. Maybe I should expand my radius."

She smiles, takes her hat off, sets it beside her. I watch her fingers as they straighten her hair, gently shape it at the back of her neck. Watch her small mouth smile.

On the sidewalk, outside, at noon, she offers her hand once again. I fold it into mine. Thoughts, cobwebs in a heat draft, float upward from recesses I have forgotten. Her skin, her hair, her mouth. A woman's hand, in mine.

But I maintain outward poise. "Thanks again, Gert."

"My pleasure."

I look around, let her hand go. "How will you get home?"

"I'll walk. It's a beautiful day."

"It is."

"And you?"

"Streetcar will take me right along Dundas to Margueretta."

She opens her purse, rummages briefly, takes out a piece of paper and a pencil, quickly scrawls something. "I'll see you next Sunday, I trust. But if you should need anything, if I can help in any way, don't hesitate to give me a ring." She hands me the paper. "And call me for a last consultation before entering the monastery." The smile.

I take my eyeglasses from my jacket pocket, slip them on, hold the scrap in both hands and read what is on it: LY 6027. A code to a new world. The threads of the spiderweb brush against my nerve ends again.

When I look up, she has already crossed Dundas and is heading down Pacific Avenue, a tiny figure. I watch her all the way to Annette before the streetcar finally slides to a halt in front of me, blocking my view.

That afternoon, Margaret phones. She and Jack want to stay with Aunt Rose for the next few days. Rose gets on the phone, assures me that this is fine with her.

I feel the pressure lift. Are you sure it's okay? I ask Rose.

Don't worry, she says. You can use the time alone. They're fine with us.

Alone, I think. But I do not want to be alone. I feel the guilt surfacing.

Don't worry, she adds again.

I appreciate this, Rose.

They're good kids, she says.

I don't know how you do it, Rose. I find them quite a handful.

Take care of yourself, Martin.

I ignore the cookbook, boil potatoes and fry some ham for dinner, wish that I had a bottle of beer to drink with my meal, like the old days, before the mad zeal of this prohibition. They say the Temperance Act will be repealed soon. Not soon enough for me.

The evening is long and warm. After eating I go out for a walk, cross St. Clarens, end up on Lansdowne, staring at the house where Maggie and I lived when the children were small. Where we lived when Jack was born. Like that night on Power Street—the day I was let go by Peter Sterling, standing on the street across from St. Paul's Church, staring through the windows above the dairy—I see people that I do not know moving about in the rooms, people like myself, who cannot see their futures, who will not be here two years or three years or five years from now.

When I come back to my flat I sit in my reading chair, but it is Sunday, there is no newspaper today, nothing to read. I light a cigar, take the piece of paper from my pocket, study it again. LY 6027. Then I fold it up, tuck it back into my pocket. Rising, I take my copy of *Sister Carrie* from the bookshelf, the only other book that I have ever purchased, and sit again in the chair, holding it in my lap like a talisman. I know much of it by heart. I know how it ends. *Know, then, that for you is neither surfeit nor content. In your rocking-chair, by your window dreaming, shall you long, alone. In your rocking-chair, by your window, shall you dream such happiness as you may never feel.*

Lying in bed later, the sheets tossed back against the heat, staring up into the darkness of the room, I begin to see, in the still, silent shadows near the ceiling, a path down which I am headed. I hear my father's voice in the night in Elora long ago, arguing futilely against the momentum that pulled him to the city, see him eating quietly at our table on Brookfield, the heels of his shoes worn down. I see Margaret Loy, my grandmother, stunned by life into an unending silence, sipping from a silver thermos held to her lips. And I know that in a darkness deeper than this by far, in a shadow I can scarcely make out, my brother Mike, no longer able to say the name Kervin aloud, is lying on white sheets, alone, helpless against the enemy, time, not knowing, not understanding that "loy" is the Irish for shovel.

I see three candles on a birthday cake—a white one, a red one, and a blue one. The white one is gone. The red one is puddled. Only the blue one remains.

Monday, after work, I dial LY 6027 and ask for Gert. We talk of her job, the weather. We talk about what we had for dinner. She asks me if I called because I am heading into the monastery and I laugh.

We do not talk of politics. That was what Maggie and I talked about. This is different. This is new. This is another chance. Maggie is gone, forever.

Wednesday evening, the phone rings. It is Gert. Would I like to come to dinner at her place Friday night? I could come there after work.

Yes. Why not. That sounds lovely.

Flustered, I forget that I have children until I hang up. Then I call Rose, tell her that I'll be busy Friday, could they stay there with her a little longer.

Busy where? You chasing the ladies already? she asks with humor.

Something I have to do, I say, caught off guard at her insight. I cannot tell if Rose is approving or disapproving of my sudden vagueness.

It's fine with me if it's all right with the children, she says. Here. Speak to Margaret.

Margaret comes on the phone, listens. There is just a touch of hesitation, a rhythm that implies something unsaid.

Then she asks if she will be with Aunt Rose over the weekend.

Is that okay? I ask.

It's fine. Everything is fine, says Margaret.

But it is not. There is something I do not understand, something I have missed. You sure?

I'll look after Jack. There's lots to do.

But I hear a new tone in her voice, a resignation with which I am unfamiliar.

Don't worry, Father. I'll help Aunt Rose.

Margaret's terrific, Rose says, back on the line. And Jack is quick as a whip.

I do not think of Jack in this way and am surprised to hear such a description. He's not giving you any trouble? I ask.

We went to hear him sing in the school choir Monday night. He sang like an angel. I almost wanted to cry, she says.

I am quiet. I had no idea he was in the choir. For a moment I am stricken speechless. I close my eyes. I know what I am doing: I am pawning off my children on my sister. Yet I cannot stop myself. I deserve a life, I think. Rose is better with them than I am.

Maybe I should talk to Margaret again.

But I do nothing. I sit there, holding the phone. My life has become what I never dreamed it could become. I am becoming what I never dreamed I would become.

Call me on the weekend. Sunday. Take care of your business, Rose says, stressing the last word wryly.

I cannot sleep, thinking of Gert.

Thursday, at lunch, I step out onto Queen for a haircut. I want to look my best tomorrow. In the barber chair, trying to calm myself, the scissors cleaning my neck, around my ears, I am filled with second thoughts. What am I doing? How old is she? What will people think?

Yet I cannot stop myself. Everything has a momentum, I realize. I am swept along.

Gert is here, Maggie is not: guilt, mixed with longing so powerful it is like a flood of madness. My mind races.

Another chance. I want another chance at life. I want it so badly, suddenly, that it scares me. The hands touching my nape, my scalp, are not the barber's. They are hers. They are Gert's. I am not forty-six. I am eighteen again, breathless, in the loft of the barn at Boyd's farm, a girl's mouth, her tongue touching mine.

Number 238 Gilmour Avenue is a reasonably new semi-detached brick house with a wooden verandah on a pretty street. I meet Mrs. McNulty and Gert's older sister, Evelyn. I can feel it: I am back in a house among women who welcome me, would take care of me. All this after so many years of knowing that I was somehow letting every-one down.

Gert and Evelyn have cooked a meal of meat loaf, po-tatoes, peas, squash. Good china is set out, frail, with small pink flowers painted on its edges, along with proper silver-ware and white cloth napkins. We drink tea after dinner. An apple pie is produced for dessert. Alcohol never appears, bootleg or otherwise. I learn that Gert is twenty-seven years old, that Evelyn is thirty-six, does the same job as her sister—a switchboard operator—only for Bell Telephone. I learn that Patrick Kelly was Mrs. McNulty's husband's name, and that he died four years ago, that she and Gert and Evelyn moved in here because it was something they could afford and because it was closer to the girls' jobs. I hear that Gert is the youngest of six, that the other four are married—two more sisters and two brothers, that one or another of them is now living in Detroit. When they ask me how old I am I falter, then tell them the truth. I am forty-six, I say. Forty-six.

They are quiet. They already know, I realize. But I see something else: I have been tested and have passed. I wonder what else they know about me, wonder about the level of gossip that encircles me, about which I know nothing.

I tell them about my job at Simpson's, about Jack and Margaret, how well they are doing in school, and how my sisters—ten of them living in the city—help me take care of them. I am, after all, a widower, a man, and what do I know about children?

They nod. This, too, they seem to understand.

I cannot bring myself to talk about Maggie. Or Mike.

I ask them if I may light a cigar. They scurry, get me an ashtray, a box of matches. I glance at Gert, catch her eye, and she smiles in return, just for me. Twenty-seven, I think, not knowing what to feel besides a long-forgotten excitement. A second chance.

I have not dated a woman for eighteen years. I do not know what to do, what is acceptable anymore. Newspapers and magazines have placed the new verbal currency at my fingertips. I have read about flappers, Oxford bags, peekaboo hats, powdering your knees, have heard "Sweet Georgia Brown" and "Baby Face." But it is not my world.

Gert is standing with me on the verandah.

Alone with her, I say something that I did not know I was going to say. "You don't want to get involved with an old guy like me." It just comes out.

She is quiet, then takes my hand. "Let's go for a walk."

* * * *

The kiss, the first kiss, of course I remember that. But what I remember is the fingers at the back of my neck, brushing the clean-shaven skin, the realization of how badly I needed a woman's touch, of the void in which I had been living, of the kindness of her mouth, giving me back a piece of the life I have lost.

Forgive me, Maggie. Please forgive me. Less than eight months. I have always been so incomplete.

Oh, Gert.

I phone her the next day, Saturday, August 21, and we agree to go to breakfast again after mass tomorrow, then head down to High Park for the afternoon. I am like a schoolboy, dizzy.

Then I phone Jock, tell him I am seeing a woman. I can hear the surprise in the silent pause that hovers. Then: good for you, old man, he tells me. Get right back on that bicycle and keep riding. Come on over to my place. I'll pour you a special Ross ale, and we won't tell the government. Tell me all about it.

We sit in the backyard of Jock's home on Wallace, just off Lansdowne, in the shade of a drooping chestnut, drinking his homemade brew. He tells me that Ford is laying men off, that sales are down twenty-five percent, Chevrolet's up forty percent. GM's Acceptance Corporation, he says, has understood the importance of time payments, while old Henry has been dragging his heels, and now they're all paying the price. The Dupont and Christie plant is closing and moving out to Victoria Park and Danforth, way the hell out in the sticks, he says. How the hell am I going to get there? he says. I'll have to move, for God's sake.

Then: how old is she?

Twenty-seven, I say.

He seems stricken for a moment. Good Lord, old man, he says, finally.

I don't know what to say.

He is quiet again. He drinks his ale. Then he looks at me, says: I envy you. He nods.

I relax.

Remember those birds we used to chase? he says. That was twenty years ago. Before we started to lose our hair. I can't figure out what happened to the years. What's she see in you anyway?

I shrug. My big job. My Cadillac. My fabulous future.

We laugh.

I have not laughed for a long time.

High Park is a dream. She puts her arm through mine and we stroll languorously. The pond, the zoo, the trails, the ice cream. I touch her face, her shoulders, her hair. Twenty years disappear. They never happened.

When I come home from work on Monday and pick up the mail, I see the envelope. With a start things fall into place. It is addressed to Miss Margaret Radey and the return address is 39 Lockwood Road. It is from Mike. Every year he sends Margaret a birthday card, and even now, especially now, he has made the effort.

Margaret's birthday was August 21. It was Saturday.

In my head there is her voice on the phone, her hesitation: *Everything is fine. I'll look after Jack. There's lots to do. I'll help Aunt Rose.*

I place the envelope on the kitchen table, sit, tilt my forehead into my fingers, close my eyes. I see myself swept along

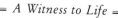

in a river, Jack and Margaret on the banks, their faces receding into the past. I do not know how any of this has happened to me, where I slipped into the current, why I cannot climb out, where I will wash up.

Seventeen

1927
1928

RADEY—McNULTY

St. Cecilia's Church was the scene of a pretty wedding on Tuesday morning, when Miss Gertrude Christine McNulty, became the bride of Mr. Martin Radey. Rev. Father Colliton officiated at the ceremony and Miss Olive Dickinson sang "O Salutaris," and "Ave Maria." The High Altar of the church was lovely with many gladioli in rose shades and tapers were burning. The bride, who was given away by her brother, Mr. Anthony McNulty, wore a gown of peach crepe romaine and a black picture hat. Her flowers were Ophelia roses and lily of the valley. Miss Evelyn McNulty was her sister's only attendant and wore a mauve georgette frock with a hat of many shades of mauve. She carried tea roses and baby's breath. Mr. Jock Ross attended the groom. After the wedding, a reception was held at the home of the bride's mother when the immediate relatives of the bride and groom joined them at wedding breakfast. Mrs. McNulty was in a gown of black georgette and wore a corsage bouquet of Richmond roses. Later in the day, Mr. and Mrs. Radey left on a wedding trip for Detroit and Cleveland. The bride traveled in a smart gown of figured georgette in tones of blue and her coat and hat were in matching shades, and her shoes of the same tone. On their return, Mr. and Mrs. Radey will reside in Toronto.

The Toronto Daily Star
Wednesday, August 10, 1927

It is September 21, the first day of autumn. In my hands I hold a crisp black-and-white photo of Gert and I standing on the verandah at 238 Gilmour, with the wedding party of ten lined up below us at the foot of the steps, all squinting into that bright, early-morning summer sunshine. I am wearing my fedora tilted rakishly forward. There are Evelyn and Jock, Gert's mother, her brother Anthony and his wife and her sister Tess and her husband. That makes seven. Only three from my side of the family stare back at me—my sister Margaret, now in her sixties, her husband John Dickinson, and their daughter Olive, my niece, who sang for us as we walked down the aisle.

That is who I see in the photo. There are people I do not see as well. I do not see my other sisters or their husbands. I do not see my more than forty other nephews and nieces.

I do not see Margaret and Jack.

My fingers squeeze the photo and I notice how the veins stand out on the back of my hands, just like Da's did.

I give up the place on Margueretta Street and move in with Gert, Evelyn, and Mrs. McNulty. Margueretta Street is another transition point, something that belongs to the past.

Margaret has graduated from high school and entered the Ontario College of Art on a scholarship. She lives with my sister Mary and Mary's husband Michael Rossiter—now that all their own family has grown up and married—back at 38 Brookfield. Jack has left school. He lives with his cousin Carmen, Mike's son, on Lockwood in the east end, and does part-time work at the gas company with him.

Gert and I rarely talk about Jack and Margaret. It is a topic we cannot solve. She does not see how they fit into my life because they do not fit into hers.

They don't need you, she says. They're almost grown up. They've got their own lives, their own friends. We need time alone. They're still upset that their mother died. I'm too young to be their mother. Time will heal the wound. They'll come around. They'll grow up and understand. What about us? What about our life?

I will lose her over them if I persist, and I cannot face this.

In the night, I cling tightly to Gert, all that I have, feel her legs wrapped about mine, breathe her warmth wildly, lose myself, again and again.

Gert is incredible. The coolness of her skin, the softness of her mouth—I am crazy about her. I tell her we need our own place, away from her sister and mother, where we can be alone. She smiles coyly, but puts me off. Wait till the spring she says. I don't want to leave Mother just yet.

Your mother will be fine. She's got Evelyn. What about us? I say, using her line. What about our life?

She comes to me, slides her hands under my jacket, along my back, kisses my chest, my neck. Spring, she says, and the fire runs through my veins as her hair, silken, dark, brushes my mouth.

BIRTHS

RADEY—At St. Joseph's Hospital, October 24, 1928, to Mr. and Mrs. Martin Radey (nee Gertrude McNulty), a daughter (Evelyn Joan).

The Toronto Daily Star
Wednesday, October 25, 1928

Eighteen

1929–32

1

GERT AND I HAVE THE UPPER DUPLEX AT 2130 DUNDAS WEST, right on the corner of Golden Avenue, our own place, finally. Joan, our daughter, is one year and six weeks old, tottering about, my new glory. She is a miracle of tiny fingers, talcum powder, eyes that shine.

It is Friday, December 6, 1929. I am reading about the president of United Cigar, whose stock plummeted on the New York Exchange from $113.50 to $4 in a single day and who jumped to his death from the ledge of his New York hotel. United Cigar stores are like Woolworth's stores, A & P, Piggly Wiggly—they are everywhere. It says that there are thirty-seven hundred of them. The paper is full of such stories. I picture him falling, the windows going by, wonder what goes through his mind in his last moments.

The phone rings and it is my sister, Mary Rossiter. She has not spoken to me for ages, so I am surprised by her call.

Martin, she says.

I wait, listen.

Do you know about Margaret? Your Margaret? she asks.

Know what? She's living with you, isn't she?

I can hear her breathing into the phone, then sighing.

She got married last Saturday, Martin. She married Tommy Nolan, Eleanor's brother.

The president of United Cigar, falling . . .

They didn't tell us. Only a few of their friends. Jack and Eleanor were the only ones there. They were married at St. Paul's.

Falling . . .

Martin? Are you there?

Margaret. Married. I am light-headed. They're just kids, I say at last. Jack and her. She's just a girl.

She's twenty years old, Martin. Tommy's twenty-five.

I hold the phone to my ear, try to picture Margaret before an altar, veiled, a bride, cannot. My little girl. My princess.

There's more, Martin. She told me yesterday. She's almost four months pregnant. The baby's expected in May.

Falling.

You're going to be a grandfather, she says.

I am floating momentarily, then dropping like a stone, unable to breathe, closing my eyes as the pavement rushes toward me.

The day that I visit Margaret in the hospital the newspapers talk of the discovery of a new planet they are calling Pluto. I am about to see my own new planet: Anne Therese Nolan, May 8, 1930. Overnight, I am an almost fifty-year-old grandfather with a one-and-a-half-year-old daughter. I hold Margaret in my arms and we cry. Then I pick up Anne, and I cry again.

Gert and Joan and I move again. There is a strangeness for me in the location of our new flat. It is like I am going in a circle. Gert and I and Joan move to 395½ Roncesvalles Avenue, an apartment atop a set of stores just north of Neepawa Avenue that has an extra room.

If I bend my neck slightly at the front window, I can see where Constance Street touches Roncesvalles. And if I close my eyes, I can see the bathroom at 10 Constance Street, Maggie lying on the floor, unbreathing, Jack and Margaret at my side.

I cannot get Jack out of my mind. Perhaps it is being a father again, seeing it all anew. Perhaps it is my age. Or maybe it is something deeper, something I can never understand.

I think of Jack singing in a choir that I have never heard.

Over the phone I ask Margaret what I want to ask her. I ask her how Jack is doing, what his phone number is.

"Where are you living?" I ask.

Jack puts the cigarette to his lips, inhales before answering. "I've got a room on Carlaw Avenue. It's near where I'm working."

I watch his eyes shine as he courts his distance, his independence. Then I say it, why I wanted to meet with him. "Come and live with us."

The smoke drifts from his mouth, his nostrils. He looks perplexed. "Come and live with who?"

"Me. And Gert and Joan."

Clouds seem to cross his face. "Why?"

"I'd like you to."

He is handsome. Nineteen years old. I see his mother's dark eyes, hair.

The windows of the coffee shop are steamed with condensation. He taps ash into a glass tray, sits back, stares at me. The smoke rises in a long tendril from the tip of the cigarette. "I don't think it would work, Father."

"We could try it."

No answer.

"Margaret thinks it's a good idea."

He looks up at me, frowns.

"Gert says it's fine with her," I say, not mentioning her list of reservations. "You'd get to know your sister."

"Margaret is my sister."

"So is Joan." I sip my coffee. "You'd get to know Gert."

His eyes turn toward the streaks of condensation running down the inside of the windows, blurring the street outside. We sit silent for a minute. Then he says: "I'm not a child anymore, Father."

I nod. "I know. Gert and I and Joan are in one room. There's a smaller room. We'd clean it out. You could have it."

"I don't know if it'd work."

I nod again. "We could try."

Silence. The smoke. The condensation. The ash grows longer, gets tapped off once more.

It is October 24, 1930, Joan's second birthday. Gert has made a cake and Joan is excited. Jack has been with us for two weeks, but we rarely see him. He comes in late, says little, stays in his room.

Dinnertime comes and Jack does not come home. It's not fair to Joan, says Gert, and I agree. Joan has been waiting all day. We eat, light the candles, let Joan blow them out, tell her that Jack had to work late.

We are in bed when we hear Jack come in. We lie in the dark and listen to him go to the icebox, run water into the sink, visit the bathroom, close the door to his room.

Jack eats with us seldom, talks little. I think that we are making some progress, but Gert says that Jack does not like her.

She thinks that he likes Joan, but he definitely does not like her, she insists.

Give him time, I say. He needs time.

I know that he is worth it. I know that the fault is mine. I know that he can sing and that I have never heard him.

It is Friday, November 28. I hear their voices as I climb the stairs to our store-top apartment.

Jack. Gert.

It is past six. I am home from work. It is the weekend. When I open the door, they both turn and stare at me, their sudden silence like a knife. In the middle, I realize again. They turn to me, in the middle, accusing. I can feel the tension.

I wait for someone to speak.

Jack glares at me, then at Gert, then goes into his room, slamming the door.

Joan is sitting in her high chair, watching, curved spoon wrapped around her hand, a bowl of applesauce before her.

"What is it?" I ask.

"Oh, Martin," Gert says, shaking her head.

"What?"

"It's Jack. He's got beer. He's been drinking."

I'm still unsure what the problem is. I don't know what I have walked in on. "Do you mean today? Now?"

"I don't know about today. He shouldn't be drinking in the house at all. He knows I disapprove. And with Joan here."

I look at Joan, who smiles. She bangs her spoon on her plate.

"I don't even know where he got it," she says. "Is it that easy to get at his age?"

I think of Jock, of Pabst Near Beer, of drinking home brew on a bench at Sunnyside, beneath the branches of the chestnut in his backyard. "He's almost twenty years old," I say, finally.

"It's against the law." Her eyes flash. "I poured it down the sink."

"Poured what?" I am not sure that I am following.

"Five bottles. I found them this morning at the back of the icebox."

"Without telling him?"

"I don't need to tell him." Her voice hardens. "This is my home. My icebox. We have a little girl here. And he brings it into our home."

"Gert—"

"You're not going to stand up for him, are you? Drinking?" Her voice is incredulous.

Jack comes out of his room, stops, stares, then walks by us toward the apartment door.

"Jack, wait." I keep my voice calm. I raise my arm, touch my temple as I try to think.

He stops.

"Where are you going?"

His hand clenches the doorknob. The muscles of his jaw work. "Away," he says. Then he looks at me, ignores Gert. "It was a mistake, Father."

No, I think. No, Jack, it wasn't. Don't go. Not now. It's just starting. We need time. "These things happen in a family," I say.

"No," he says. "No, they don't." He looks from one to the other of us. "Not in a real family."

"Gert didn't mean—"

"Yes I did. I don't want it in the house."

Jack straightens, looks at me. "Mother would never have done this," he says. "Have you forgotten?"

I am stung. It is as though my face has been slapped. I have not forgotten. I can never forget.

He looks at me, controls his breathing. "What have you done?" he asks, with finality. Then: "Why did you do it?"

I don't know. I don't know why anybody does anything, why anything happens. There is an actual physical ache in my chest. Parts of me are sliding away, breaking up. I feel his contempt, his anger, a wind blowing hotly. "Don't be so hard on me, Jack," I say. "Don't be so hard on Gert either."

"You're not hard enough on yourself, Father."

"Don't be rude to your father," says Gert.

Jack looks at her. "Rude?" he says, amazed. His eyes linger on her, puzzled.

Joan bangs her spoon on her tray. Her eyes are wide. "Jack," I say.

But the door opens, then closes, and he is gone.

2

[File Card, MOUNT HOPE CEMETERY:]

Anthony Nolan died ___11 March 1931___
buried ___19 March 1931___
stillborn _____
St. Michael's Hospital
funeral director ___Connors___
single grave 46
section ___10___
range _4_

Margaret's son. My grandson. I think of little Patrick and Loretta, so many years ago, in the ground at Elora. And Sarah, Da, Gramma, Kervin, Liz, Ma, Maggie, Mike.

Anthony.

Jack.

* * * *

Wednesday, March 2, 1932, the newspaper headline shouts:

LINDBERGH BABY KIDNAPPED
Taken From Crib
Wide Search On

A family photo appears below, showing the baby, Charles Augustus Lindbergh, Jr., surrounded by his mother, grandmother, and great-grandmother. A ransom note has been left. It is unbelievable. That anyone could do such a thing.

The world is crazy, I think suddenly. Someone is going into other people's houses and taking children. They are just disappearing.

Margaret and Tommy and Anne live with Tommy's parents. The Nolans have moved from Berkeley Street to a new semi-detached house in the north end of the city, on Maxwell Avenue, near Yonge and Eglinton. Margaret has found a home, a life, made her own family with another family.

I am not sure what to make of Tommy. I have trouble talking with the man who got my Margaret pregnant before he married her. And he has trouble talking to me. His parents, too, have treated me coolly the few times I have visited, and I wonder what they have been told. Tommy plays guitar and banjo in bands all around the city, plays out-of-town jobs, plays in orchestras at the King Edward, the Palais Royale, plays jobs on the Island and with Romanelli's Orchestra on the cruise boats that sail across the lake to Niagara and back in the evenings.

But Margaret has recovered from the stillbirth. She is pregnant again. There will be another baby in November.

Art school is a memory.

*   *   *   *

KNIGHTS OF COLUMBUS
HOLD SWAY AT ISLAND
Afternoon's Big Event
at Annual Picnic
is Baby Show

More than 2,500 members of the Toronto council, Knights of Columbus, yesterday flocked across Toronto Bay to Center Island for the council's annual picnic.

During the afternoon there was a long list of sports. Despite the heavy downpour, the afternoon was its usual successful self. One of the big events of the afternoon was the baby show, which was justified with some forty entries, out of which the judges had difficulty in awarding final results.

The grand winner of the sweepstake was Anne Therese Nolan, 2-year-old daughter of Mr. and Mrs. Thomas Nolan, adjudged the bonniest baby in the show. Anne was presented with a handsome sterling silver porringer.

The Evening Telegram
August 10, 1932

I watch as Gert shows the picture of Anne that accompanies the newspaper piece to Joan, who is almost four years old, and who is fascinated by the idea of a baby contest.

Joan's finger rests on Anne's face, against her cheek.

"That's your niece," Gert explains. "You're her aunt. Aunt Joan."

Joan looks at her mother, smiles. "Aunt Joan," she says.

At Woolworth's we buy a flat five-by-four-inch congratulations card:

> *On this happy occasion*
> *I want to help you celebrate*
> *by sending my Best Wishes.*

On it is a house, sitting lushly amidst an array of chocolate and pink flowers. In the bottom right-hand corner, in fine print, is scrolled: *Etching, Genuine Hand Colored.*

Gert addresses the envelope to Miss Anne Nolan, signs the card "Joan Radey." She lets Joan lick the brown two-cent George V stamp and place it in the upper right corner of the envelope.

Gert lifts her up as she drops it in the mail slot.

I watch in amazement, as she sends it across the city, to my daughter, my granddaughter. Children everywhere, I think.

Specters of Patrick, Loretta, Anthony float in some dark recess. Then I shake my head, trying to lose another image that has surfaced: it has been three months since baby Lindbergh's body was found, decomposing in the woods some four miles from the family's estate.

Margaret calls on October 24 and puts Anne on the phone to wish Joan a happy fourth birthday. When I get the chance, I make conversation, ask her if she's following the Lindbergh story.

Isn't everybody? she asks. It's unbelievable. How could anyone do such a thing?

But I am not good at small talk, so I ask her what I am avoiding asking, what I carry around inside me like a stone. I ask her if she knows where Jack is.

She tells me that Jack is gone, that he and his cousin Carmen have left the country, gone to Detroit to look for work in the auto industry, that they heard there were jobs there. Don't worry, Father, she says. He's written a couple of letters. He moves around, but I have a few addresses. He'll keep in touch.

On November 21, Margaret and Tommy become parents again—a brother for Anne. My grandson, Ronald Francis, is born in the back bedroom of the Nolan house on Maxwell Avenue. Margaret is fine. The baby is healthy.

Before Christmas, Gert and Joan and I move to an apartment atop stores at 3097A Dundas West, just east of Clendenan. The new place is a better fit, cheaper, since we no longer need Jack's room.

I do not tell Gert about how I could see Constance Street from our front window, about how I could not stop myself from looking, about how it is better if we go.

Nineteen

1934

AUGUST, 1934. JOAN CARRIES A BOX OF HER TOYS UP THE stairs beside me at 265 Pacific Avenue. She is five years old, almost six, has long black hair curling to her shoulders, a white bow tied at the top of her head.

"Which room is mine?" she asks, large eyes peering through the open door of the new flat.

"Last one on the left."

She scampers ahead. I listen as the box is set down, hear the closet door being opened for inspection.

Gert, who has been climbing the stairs behind me, appears now at my side. Winded, smiling, she clutches my arm.

Our new flat is in a lovely, brick, three-storey detached house on the northeast corner of Pacific and Humberside. We are only eight blocks from Gert's mother and sister on Gilmour, five blocks from St. Cecilia's School where Joan will start grade one in September. It is tree lined, a residential street—the complete opposite of Dundas—where Joan can play more safely.

It was down Pacific Avenue that I watched Gert disappear

that first day, that Sunday, before the streetcar pulled in front of me, blocking her from sight. Now Gert squeezes my arm, lets me know her pleasure. I look at her face staring up at mine, realize how pale and tired she seems. I put my arm around her shoulder, pull her tight, think how a man needs a family, how I need her.

"You did well," says Jock, glancing around the new place.

"Considering," I say.

"Pardon?"

"Considering my wages have been cut thirty percent. And that this is smaller than where we were by three hundred square feet."

"Beautiful house, though. Beautiful street." Jock pauses, thinks. Then: "Thirty percent?"

I nod.

"That's a whack."

"At least I still have a job. They say one in five is unemployed." I look at him. "Did you hear that Metropolitan Life Insurance now claims there were twenty thousand suicides in thirty-one?"

Jock looks surprised, mulls this over. Finally, he says, "There's talk of closing down the Victoria Park and Danforth plant."

I turn and look at him. He is talking about where he works, the place he must travel to every morning, halfway across the city. This is the first I have heard of it. "What do you mean?"

"Just talk."

"Anything to it?"

He shrugs. "Don't know. I hear the talk, though. Hear that it'll be phased out. Replaced as a Nash assembly plant."

I am quiet.

"You seen the pictures in the papers of them Bennett buggies—cars hitched up to teams of horses, 'cause folks can't afford to put gas in 'em?"

I nod. "I've seen them."

"We laughed at first." A beat. "Nobody's laughin' now."

"You heard of Hoover blankets? Hoover flags?" I ask.

Jock waits, a wry smile.

"The blankets are old newspapers to cover yourself up with on the park bench. The flags are empty pockets turned inside out."

We share a dry chuckle.

"Bennett, Hoover, Roosevelt. None of them can get the job done. None of them know what to do," I say.

"Hoover was a Quaker. Pacifist. Didn't know how to fight. Didn't know what he was up against. Bennett'll be out on his ass here next election. He only got in because Mackenzie King was in the wrong place at the wrong time. Wheat prices were a disaster, and there he is, sittin' in Ottawa, and everybody looks at him. King'll be back, you wait and see. Roosevelt? Well, he talks a good game. They all talk a good game."

We stand in the half-filled flat, collect our breath, think about the boxes and chairs and disassembled beds and lamps and even the washing machine still outside on the front lawn. Joan's old wicker pram is in the corner, filled with small dresses, blouses, shoes, and the Shirley Temple doll Margaret bought for her after she took Joan and Anne to see her in *Stand Up and Cheer*. I take two cigars from my vest pocket and hand one to Jock. We light them, smoke them in silence, enjoying the moment, unable to see the future, as always.

"Why do I have to go to school?" asks Joan.

"So you can learn to read." Gert is clearing the table, filling the sink with water.

Joan, lying on her stomach on the floor, has the funny

pages of the newspaper spread open in front of her. "I can already read." She points to a bubble of dialogue near her elbow. "What does 'Leapin' Lizards!' mean?"

Gert turns to me. It is Friday, August 31.

I place my cigar in the ashtray, lean forward, look at Joan's tiny finger pressed against the black and white of the comic strip. "Where is it?" I ask.

"It's what Little Orphan Annie says all the time."

"It's just an expression."

"Why do they have no eyes?"

"It's just the way they draw them."

Her feet are in the air, moving back and forth.

"You'll make new friends at school. Tell her, Mother." I turn to Gert.

But Gert is pale, clutching her stomach.

"Gert."

She turns, looks at me. Her face is ashen. "Martin," she says. "There's something wrong." There is a sheen of perspiration on her forehead and upper lip. Her eyes are distant, pleading.

No, I think. I rise up out of my chair, go to her, hold her by the shoulders. Not Gert. I have seen this all before, somewhere. This is impossible. "What is it?"

Joan looks up, her face a mask.

"I don't know. Something's wrong. Stomach cramps. Pain."

"Lie down. I'll finish cleaning up." I hold her by the shoulders, afraid to let her see my fear, my desperation. Afraid to let her go. Not Gert, I am still thinking. Please God. Not Gert.

Joan watches in silence. Her feet have stopped moving.

I am waiting in the kitchen as the doctor comes out of the bedroom. Joan is down the hall, in bed.

He sets his bag down on the table, looks at me. "I'm going to put her in the hospital," he says.

"Why? What's the matter?"

"How old is your wife?"

"Thirty-five," I say. "Why?"

"I think she's pregnant, Mr. Radey. And I'm afraid something's wrong."

"Pregnant?" It is like a wind rushing over me. Another baby, I think. The wind is hot, then cold. My right hand clutches and rubs my left shoulder, kneading a muscle that has cramped. "I didn't know she was pregnant," I manage, finally, foolishly.

"I don't think she knew either."

Pregnant, I think. A child. I am fifty-four. "What do you mean something's wrong? What's wrong?"

"She might be miscarrying. She's hemorrhaging. Do you have a phone?"

The questions dizzy me, come at me from an echo chamber: how old is she? do you have a phone? I have heard them before, in another life.

I point to the phone, speechless.

> RADEY—At St. Michael's Hospital, on Sunday, September 2nd, Gertrude McNulty, dearly beloved wife of Martin Radey.
>
> Funeral from her sister's home, Mrs. J. Mahoney, 75 Fairview Avenue, on Tuesday to St. Cecilia's Church for Mass at 10 A.M.
>
> Interment in Mount Hope Cemetery.
>
> *The Globe and Mail*
> *Tuesday, September 4, 1934*

*   *   *   *

What do you mean dead? I shout. How could she be dead? You don't die from a miscarriage. This is impossible.

I knock the glasses off my face as I stumble about, thrashing at the hospital curtains surrounding her bed.

Where is her doctor? My voice is loud, too loud, but I cannot control it. I cannot control anything. The muscles in my bladder have had a momentary spasm and my leg is wet. The room is blurred. Gert is here, in this room, but dead.

I want to see her doctor.

He's not on duty this weekend. The nurse is red faced.

What do you mean, not on duty? I sputter. What are you telling me? Are you telling me he was off golfing somewhere while my wife was dying? Is that what you're telling me? He's fishing somewhere?

Mr. Radey. Mr. Radey. Please. We understand. Please.

Understand? How could you understand? I don't understand. You bring that goddamn doctor to me, you hear me? I want to talk to him now.

People gather in the hall, looking into the room, quiet, trying to see what is going on. Someone inside closes the door.

This can't be happening, I shout. It can't.

Mr. Radey. Please.

I want to see the doctor. Bring that fucking doctor to me. Now! How did she die? Tell me how she died.

Septicemia, someone says. I hear the word, then it flutters in the air like a moth, heads for the flame.

I don't know what that is. What the hell is septicemia? What are you telling me?

Septic poisoning. Blood poisoning.

Why wasn't she helped? Why wasn't she given something? There are things she could have been given. Where was her doctor all weekend?

Someone touches my shoulder. It's the Labor Day weekend, Mr. Radey. People are away. We're a bit short staffed.

My wife died because it's a holiday weekend? Is that what you're fucking telling me? Is that it?

No, Mr. Radey. Please. We understand.

The room spins. I clutch at an intern's sleeve. Somebody holds me from behind. My eyes are wet and I still do not have my glasses on. Don't Mr. Radey me! I shout, spittle flying from my lips. Who's in charge here? I want to talk to whoever's in charge. Get me somebody in here right now. Get me fucking somebody who will explain this to me for Christ's sake!

On the day that Joan is to start school she attends her mother's funeral instead. I lift her in my arms and carry her with me as we get out of our cars in the cemetery and I do not put her down but hold her tightly, her arms about my neck, keeping her close, not letting her go, because, incredibly, suddenly, she is all that I have.

My life with Jack and Margaret is over. Gone. I can never get it back. I can never undo my neglect, my selfishness. I was unwilling to pay the price of parenting.

It will not happen again. I will not let it.

Twenty

The valley is dark and beautifully wet. You can almost see the grass growing and the leaves pushing out of the poplars. There are small flowers on my redbuds and the dogwood buds are beginning to swell.

—THOMAS MERTON
A Vow of Conversation: Journals 1964–1965

DEATH WAS LIKE LIFE: A SERIES OF SURPRISES THAT IN HINDSIGHT were not surprises. The simplest things happened over and over again, forever catching me off guard. Death occurred daily, here, in the past, below in life, everywhere.

Since morning, three starlings have toppled off branches into the tall grasses below. Yesterday, four were killed on the railway tracks that skirt the lake. The sky was filled with birds, singly and in flocks, tunneling through the air in every direction, destinations inbred or random.

And the hawk, always above us, always circling just beyond sight, dropped among us on a daily basis, a sleek bolt exploding in a small burst of feathers, then silence.

Picture us sitting in a grand maple tree, a hundred, two hundred, the incessant squealing, squawking. Then, as before, as always, we rose up in a cloud of shimmering ink blots, without sound, the world, patchwork, spread out below us.

Again, in the wind: into the soft spots, the loops, the silky linings of time, where everything existed, equal.

Southwest, across the years, across the miles, sifting through the millions that would die amidst rubble, mud, on water, interred and disposed of and bulldozed over in ways beyond imagining, I saw the denouement, the path to the monk's cell down which we all wind.

Twenty-one

1934–1950

1

Joan and I move into 238 Gilmour Avenue with Gert's sister, Evelyn, and Mrs. McNulty. It is, I vow, my last move.

I refuse to pay Gert's doctor bill and am slowly dunned with notices, finally threatened with legal action. But when the doctor himself phones one evening to discuss the matter, the rage rises inside me like a volcano and I spew a lava of vitriol that causes my hands to shake and my vision to blur.

I never hear from him again.

On Christmas Day, 1935, Gert's mother, Mrs. McNulty, dies.

Joan is learning how people disappear, how plans slip away, how things spin off into chaos. But she is learning it much too young—as I did—and I feel helpless to protect her.

The house has been left to Evelyn, with the understanding that Joan and I live here too.

I will not move. I can never move again. Moving, I now believe, must have been part of the bad luck that has stalked me through the years.

We stay at 238 Gilmour. Evelyn helps with Joan, with

meals, and in this modest house where three women—two of whom are now gone—made me welcome nine years ago, I try to hold onto the thread of my life.

Evelyn suggests moving Joan's bed to Mrs. McNulty's empty room, but I ignore her, keep it in the corner of my room.

I keep it there because I must. I must know where she is. I cannot lose her. I think that just knowing that she is nearby, in the darkness, is enough. But I wake her with my nightmares on a regular basis, and I know that for this reason, and so many others, Evelyn is right, she must have her own space, soon.

In the evening of April 3, 1936, at the Trenton State Prison death house, which measures eleven feet by twenty-three feet, fifty-seven people witness the execution of Bruno Richard Hauptmann in the electric chair, for the kidnapping and murder of Charles Augustus Lindbergh, Jr., four years earlier. To the end, Hauptmann proclaims his innocence.

After one last nightmare, Evelyn helps me move Joan down the hall, into her own room, finally.

It is 1938 and Roosevelt becomes the first U.S. president to visit Canada while in office, meeting with Mackenzie King in Kingston, Ontario. Jock and I, the Orangeman and the Catholic, discuss this knowledgeably in chairs beneath the chestnut tree in his backyard. His daughter, Gail, twenty-one married, with a daughter of her own, is visiting.

Joan is almost ten. She is by my side. She is always by my side.

On June 7, 1939, married almost ten years, Margaret and Tommy have a third child, a daughter, Judith Rita. My second granddaughter.

Late July, cabbage and potatoes boiling on the stove, Evelyn slumps to the floor of our kitchen and, hands shaking, I call an ambulance. A stroke. I cannot believe it. Maggie, Gert, Mrs. McNulty, now Evelyn. All the women I try to live with.

In August, when she returns from the hospital, Evelyn, suddenly old, now needing the help that she has given me, walks with a chair and is confined to the main floor.

September 3, 1939, Britain and France declare war on Germany. A week later, Canada joins them.

It is a gray, wintry Saturday afternoon in December, a light snow beginning to fall, a damp cold pervading, when the RCMP come to the door looking for Jack Radey. He has not answered a draft notice of some kind. I tell them that I do not know where he is. I tell them that no one knows where he is.

I am sixty, sixty-one, sixty-two, going on sixty-three.

In 1940 I stand at the same graveside twice: January 27, my sister Kate dies. Six months later, her husband, Jim Bedford, follows her.

December 7, 1941. Pearl Harbor. The United States declares war. My sister Teresa's boy, Ed, is missing in action somewhere in the Pacific theater.

Tuesday, September 1, 1942, Joan starts high school at Western Commerce, just south of Annette Street. I have made our dinner tonight: what Joan calls my famous chicken casserole. It will be her turn to cook tomorrow.

"Should I take science or music?"

I am placing the cutlery on the table when she asks, and I look up. "You have a choice?"

"If you join the band you don't have to take science. Music class is at the same time."

"But then you'd have to take it next year."

"I guess."

"Postponing the inevitable."

She is silent.

"Do you want to join the band?"

"Not really."

"Then why the question?"

"You'd want to join the band too if you'd met my science teacher today like I did. He's weird. He made us sit there for twenty minutes without saying a word after lecturing us for the first half of the period. He never smiled. Not once. He's scary."

I pull my chair out, sit down. "What's his name?"

"Mr. Zoltan. Even his name is weird. He's got black greasy hair. Yuk."

"What instrument would you play if you joined the band? I can't picture you with a tuba."

She thinks. "Maybe the clarinet. Or the flute."

I nod. "It seems like a strange choice."

"The clarinet?"

"No. Science or joining the band."

She is staring at me, listening intently.

"Maybe you should give it another week, then see how you feel about it."

She looks doubtful, picks up her fork, pokes at her food.

"Then, if you still want to switch, I'll go in with you and help you get it done."

She looks at me hopefully.

"I'll take the morning off."

"You will? Promise?"

"Promise."

She smiles.

"I forgot to get us something to drink," I say, realizing that our glasses are empty.

"I'll get it," she says, rising suddenly, animated, going to the refrigerator.

She pours the milk into her glass and opens the bottle of cold beer with a snap. After she pours it for me, she gives me a quick peck on the forehead. "Maybe the flute," she says. Her smile, given freely, is what I want, what I need. I know now, I think, where the thermometer is, where the spare blankets are. I know her birthday.

We listen to Jack Benny on the radio in the evening as a respite from news of the war in Europe and the Pacific.

By November, Mr. Zoltan is one of Joan's favorite teachers. She has an A in science.

In 1945, what happened to Kate and Jim happens to my sister Margaret and her husband. January 19, age eighty, Margaret, always in my corner, dies. On May 13, John Dickinson joins her.

Then Hiroshima. Nagasaki. August 1945. I do not understand what has happened, what kind of weapon they have devised, but it is over, at last.

Joan, sixteen, going on seventeen, is with her friends downtown. They are dancing in the streets, riding up Yonge Street on hoods of cars, horns honking.

Ed, Teresa's son, comes home. It is a miracle. A big man who once weighed close to two hundred pounds, he now weighs eighty. The war for him was years in a Japanese camp on an island whose name he says he cannot remember. He tells us stories—how they once were so hungry that they coaxed a stray dog close to the wire fence that was the edge of their world, how they killed it, cooked it, made soup, how it kept them alive.

It has been almost fifteen years since I have seen Jack, since I have seen my son, since that night in November of 1930 when the door closed and he disappeared down the stairs, out of my life. Margaret has shown me the last letter he wrote to her. It was from the Scott Hotel, Ashland, Kentucky, postmarked July 1, 1934.

Then, silence. It haunts me. The world has waged a war to end all wars, and now must rebuild entire cities, entire countries. Maybe I can dredge through the rubble. Maybe it is not too late. I did not know that he could sing. I never heard him.

2

MARGARET HAS LENT ME THE CORRESPONDENCE THAT SHE RE-ceived from Jack—faded envelopes with green, red, and purple Washington stamps, and addresses that failed even Edwards Investigation Services. They are all from 1934.

The contents are spread out on the table in front of me. Four letters: the first from the Vermont Hotel, 138 W. Columbia, Detroit; another from 117 Seventeenth Street, Toledo, Ohio; a third from a place called the Highway, Bucyrus, Ohio; and the final one from the Scott Hotel, Ashland, Kentucky.

I arrange the sheets of yellowed hotel stationery into neat piles, runes, an archaeological dig, reading and rereading them, searching for something overlooked, a starting place. They are lengthy: four sheets, double sided, from Detroit ("Phone Cherry 4421, Rates $1.00 and up"); two sheets, double sided, from Toledo; three sheets, single sided this time ("Modern, Fireproof, In the Heart of Bucyrus on the Lincoln Highway"); then a final torn sheet from Ashland, Kentucky ("Fire Proof, Moderate Price, Tub and Shower Baths"). But what I see, what jumps out at me, what leaves me dry mouthed and trembling is a threefold repetition.

Toledo: *Say hello to Father and all the gang for me, and write* me sooner than I did you. Try and forgive me for not writing sooner—cause you know how a fellow slips once in a while.

Bucyrus: *Let me know how Father is getting along. I've lost his address.*

Ashland: *Say Hello to Father for me.*

Edwards Investigation Services
212 Spadina Avenue, suite 100
Toronto, Ontario
May 22, 1946

Martin Radey
238 Gilmour Avenue
Toronto, Ontario

Dear Mr. Radey:

Pursuant to the discussion in our office yesterday and your acceptance of our fee structure, we are agreeing to undertake a search for your son, John Francis (Jack) Radey. We would, however, like to state a few facts as a matter of record before beginning.

As I told you, an estimated 1 million people are reported missing—in both the United States and Canada combined—every year. More than 150,000 of these never return home or contact family again. It has been our experience that most of them want to be missing, that this is their choice. As you can imagine, the recent war in the Pacific and Europe has only complicated matters further.

If this is the case with your son, we can offer no guarantees other than our assurance as professionals that we will pursue each logical avenue of recourse at your specific direction.

As mentioned during our discussion, we believe the United States military is the logical place to begin a search.

Sincerely,
Simon Paul Edwards
(President)

Edwards Investigation Services
212 Spadina Avenue, suite 100
Toronto, Ontario
May 25, 1946

Martin Radey
238 Gilmour Avenue
Toronto, Ontario

Dear Mr. Radey:

I am sending you a copy of the letter that was mailed, as per your instructions, to the Regional Offices of the Veterans Administration for the states of Michigan, Indiana, Ohio, Illinois, Pennsylvania, New York, New Jersey, Delaware, West Virginia, Kentucky, Missouri, Maryland, Connecticut, Virginia, Massachusetts and California (sixteen states in all).

In the event that John F. Radey may still be in the armed forces, I have also sent slightly modified copies of the inquiry to the following agencies:

- US Army Personnel Service Support Center
  Fort Benjamin Harrison, Indiana

- Air Force Military Personnel Center
  Randolph AFB
  San Antonio, Texas

- Navy Annex Building
  Washington, DC

- *Marine Corps Headquarters*
  Washington, DC

- *US Coast Guard*
  2100 2nd Street, SW
  Washington, DC

- *Retired Military and Civil Service Personnel*
  1900 E. Street, SW
  Washington, DC

- *General Services Administration*
  National Personnel Records Center
  9700 Page Blvd.
  St. Louis, Missouri

Director, Regional Office
Veterans Administration
(regional office address)
(date)

Re: John Francis (Jack) Radey
Date of Birth: April 30, 1911
Place of Birth: Toronto, Ontario, Canada

Dear Sir:

I have an urgent reason for contacting the above individual. If he is in your file and you have a current address, would you please forward to him the enclosed stamped, unaddressed postcard. If you have no record of him, would you please return the postcard to me for my records.

Sincerely,
etc.

[POSTCARD]

DEAR JACK:
I ASKED THE VA TO FORWARD THIS CARD AS I HAVE NO IDEA WHERE YOU ARE AND WOULD LIKE TO HEAR FROM YOU. PLEASE WRITE (238 GILMOUR AVE, TORONTO) OR CALL COLLECT (LY 6027).
FATHER

Edwards Investigation Services
212 Spadina Avenue, suite 100
Toronto, Ontario
July 8, 1946

Martin Radey
238 Gilmour Avenue
Toronto, Ontario

Dear Mr. Radey:
As it has been six weeks since the first steps of our investigation into the whereabouts of your son, John F. Radey, and since we have had no positive response as yet, I recommend that we proceed with the next phase of the search. To this end, I have enclosed a copy of the letter we discussed over the phone, addressed to the US Social Security Administration.

Director, Locator Service
Social Security Administration
6401 Security Blvd.
Baltimore, Maryland

Re: John Francis (Jack) Radey
Date of Birth: April 30, 1911
Place of Birth: Toronto, Ontario, Canada

Dear Sir:

I have an urgent humanitarian reason for contacting the above individual. If he is in your file and you have a current address for him, would you please forward to him the enclosed, stamped, unaddressed postcard*. If you have no record of him, would you please return the postcard to me for my records.

Sincerely,
etc.

(*postcard will be a modified version of one previously used)

Edwards Investigation Services
212 Spadina Avenue, suite 100
Toronto, Ontario
September 18, 1946

Martin Radey
238 Gilmour Avenue
Toronto, Ontario

Dear Mr. Radey:

In response to your written query of September 15/46, in order to request a death or marriage certificate it is required to know the state or county of the individual's residence at the time of death or marriage. Since we do not know your son's residence, this would prove a very inefficient and costly way to proceed with the search, with no guarantee of success.

American Federal Records are the ones that we can pursue with the greatest possibility of discovery of some sort. Consequently, we recommend the following sequence:

1) US District Court, which handles civil and criminal matters, and which has retrievable records;

2) Bankruptcy Court, which contains public information which is accessible by mail;

3) US Marshal, in conjunction with the National Crime Information Center (NCIC) in Washington;

4) Prison Records.

Your suggestion that we contact the US Internal Revenue Service is a sound one, but in order for them to retrieve information they require a Social Security Number, which we have been unable to obtain.

I await your written instructions before proceeding with the searches named above.

Sincerely,
Simon Paul Edwards
(President)

Edwards Investigation Services
212 Spadina Avenue, suite 100
Toronto, Ontario
December 12, 1946

Martin Radey
238 Gilmour Avenue
Toronto, Ontario

Dear Mr. Radey:
It is with deep regret that we close the file on our professional association, bringing to a halt our unsuccessful search for your son, but we do so at your instruction. You are indeed right when you say that it is a process that could go on for years, and that one must be realistic about the costs involved.

Since you may wish to pursue the issue further by yourself, while naturally minimizing costs, might we suggest contacting the Salvation Army. As well as its better-known services, it also has a Missing Persons Service. We recommend using the same letter-of-inquiry and postcard tandem that we have used on your behalf.

There are four headquarters to which you might write:

1) Eastern US: 120 W. 14th St., New York, NY
2) Central US: 860 N. Dearborn St., Chicago, Illinois
3) Southern US: 1424 NE Expressway, Atlanta, Georgia
4) Western US: 30840 Hawthorne Blvd., Rancho Palos Verdes, California

Our very best wishes for success in your search. I wish we could have had a successful conclusion to our endeavor. If we can be of further assistance, do not hesitate to contact us.

A final invoice is being prepared and will be issued shortly.

Sincerely,
Simon Paul Edwards
(President)

3

STAFF NEWS, January 23, 1948

Martin Radey of the seventh floor receiving department was the center of attraction recently when the members of the staff gathered to present him with a handsome smoking stand, cigars, and a hassock on the occasion of his retirement from the Company. Mr. Radey had been with the Company over 30 years and retired under Simpson's Retirement Security Plan.

ANN DISAPPROVES OF MY CIGAR, BUT I LIGHT IT ANYWAY, strong aromatic smoke filling the air. *The Saturday Evening Post* rests on my lap, the cover a Norman Rockwell painting of a neighborhood scene—kids playing tag, laundry hanging on lines, a man hammering shingles onto a roof.

Ann Jackson, who once worked on the switchboard at the Bell with Evelyn, now lives with us as live-in help. Evelyn's needs are more than I can handle, and Joan, herself working full-time at nineteen, cannot be tied to her either.

Joan has ended up, much like her mother, exactly like Evelyn and Ann, working switchboard at the Bell too. Even so, Joan and Ann do not get along. Ann does not understand Frank Sinatra, jukeboxes, roller rinks. Joan is strong, smart, with a mind of her own. Like Gert.

I let a stream of blue smoke float toward the green-patterned wallpaper that surrounds me. I do not know how much more time I have. Jack, I think. Jack.

I see him cross the room of the apartment atop the stores on Roncesvalles, see his hand on the doorknob, see his eyes, blue, accusing me, hear his footsteps on the stairs.

The atlas lies open on my lap, the United States stretching across two pages, topography of greens, oranges, yellows at my fingertips. I push my eyeglasses down on my nose, peer through the bottom of the lenses.

So many places. He could be anywhere.

I do not know how to start. It is overwhelming.

Detroit. Toledo. Bucyrus. Ashland.

Heading south. Disappearing like winter runoff into soft loam, sinking into the earth.

I do not understand Jack. I do not understand anyone who can travel so far, so freely. Yet I try to make the leap, try to imagine the places named before me, however ordinary they may be.

I am sixty-eight years old, past the age of discovery and experiment, born in another era, another world. Nevertheless, I am intrigued by the litany of names that Jack has evoked: Detroit, Toledo, Bucyrus, Ashland.

Ashland. Kentucky. The source of his final words.

Simon Paul Edwards and his Investigation Services have checked these places out, found nothing.

And yet.

And yet, when I close my eyes I can see Jack in some mythical Kentucky, by the side of a road, in a diner with a cigarette and coffee, leaning on the hood of a Chevy, that smile, so white, so wry.

There is a story surrounding everyone, some traces of information that are part fancy, part fact, a tale that gets passed around as casually as discussion of the weather. *Her father was a drunk. His sister committed suicide. Their mother went mad. He's worth a quarter of a million dollars.*

After mass on Sunday, the new young priest, Father Morrison, stops me outside to introduce himself. He has been at St. Cecilia's for more than a year now, since Father Colliton died, but this is the first time we have spoken. And as we talk I come to realize that there is a story surrounding me, of which I have been unaware. He tells me that someone has mentioned that I have a son living down in the States, and he asks how he is.

I see Jack smiling, cigarette in hand, the Ohio River behind him wide and deep.

He's in Kentucky, I say, surprising myself.

Kentucky? Really? What's he doing?

Operates his own business.

Father Morrison's eyes crinkle in the morning sunshine.

Hotel business, I say. Ashland.

He nods, looks around, thinking.

Ever been to Kentucky? I ask him.

As a matter of fact, I have. There's a Trappist monastery near Bardstown. Gethsemani. I was on a retreat there during my novitiate. Beautiful place. Lovely. Acres of countryside.

He looks at me.

You should go, he says. They have a guest house. A wonderful way to renew inner resources, make peace with oneself.

As I pull my hat low over my eyes, look into his face, try to determine what is there, see only concern, honesty, I hear myself talking to Gert in the restaurant on Dundas Street, that Sunday morning, more than twenty years ago. *I'm thinking of being a monk . . . It's not such a bad deal.*

You never know, I say. A pause. Nice talking with you, Father.

Same, he says, and we clasp hands.

At night, I spread the letters out on the kitchen table, touch them, reread them. Then I study the map of Kentucky that is open in the atlas beside them. Ashland is in the northeastern part of the state. Bardstown is about a hundred miles to the west, maybe thirty miles south of Louisville.

But Gethsemani, the Trappist monastery, is as invisible on my map as it must be silent. I touch the map, feel for it. I listen.

* * * *

I have never had so much time alone. Retired less than six months, I wonder what I have done with all those years. They are gone, a blur.

Gethsemani, I think. I know the name from the Bible: the garden where Christ went to pray before He was crucified.

Somewhere in Kentucky.

July 1948 is humid, even sultry. The house traps the heat, especially in the upstairs bedrooms. As I lie in my bed, hands behind my head, staring up into the darkness, I think about my resolution for the first week of August. I am planning what I have never done before. At my age, I am undertaking a trip by myself, out of the city. Five days.

I am going to Gethsemani. One day to travel there, one day to travel back, and three days at the monastery. I have phoned ahead, made the arrangements to stay in the guest house. The bus from Toronto will take me through Detroit, Toledo, Dayton, Cincinnati, Louisville. At Louisville, I transfer to a bus to Bardstown, and from there the short last leg of my journey.

When the bus rolls through Detroit and Toledo, I imagine Jack walking the streets that I see through the window, his hands in his pockets. When we pass a roadside diner outside Troy, Ohio, I conjure him up at a booth inside, a sandwich and coffee in front of him, cigarette burning in a glass ashtray. On the platform in Louisville, I see him leaning against a telephone pole, reading a newspaper. In Bardstown, he floats, for a fathomless moment, behind the wheel of a Dodge roadster that has pulled into the gas station across the street. Smiling that smile.

4

WITHIN THE WALLS ARE A SILENT HERD OF MEN, YOUNG AND old, white cowls, brown capes. At a large desk in the entranceway I am greeted by an older man in monk's garb and signed in, all talk at a minimum.

There are twenty rooms in the guest house. My room is as one might imagine: a single bed, a chair, a writing desk, two lamps. A crucifix is the sole adornment on the walls. My second-story window opens onto a closed quadrangle.

I set my bag down on the uncarpeted floor, sit on the bed, read the card that was handed to me:

A MONK'S DAY

3:00 A.M.	Rise
3:15	Choral prayer of Vigils
	Personal prayer
	Breakfast
5:45	Choral prayer of Lauds
6:15	Daily Eucharist
	Thanksgiving/Meditation
7:30	Choral prayer of Terce
8:50–11:50	Work
12:15 P.M.	Choral prayer of Sext
12:30	Dinner
	Rest/Reading/Personal Prayer
2:15	Choral prayer of None
	Reading/Personal prayer/Work
5:30	Choral prayer of Vespers
6:00	Supper/Reading/Personal Prayer
7:30	Compline (Choral night prayers)
	Retire

Guest are invited to join in any of the above activities, but are completely welcome to structure their own time to avail themselves of any of the monastery's facilities. We also encourage exploration of the natural beauty of our acreage as an aid to silent contemplation.

Standing in the monks' cemetery of miniature white crosses, there is a clean smell of pine and cedar that blows from the nearby woods. The fields are green, dotted with birches, poplars, the valley lush, hemmed in by the low, distant mountains.

At night the sky is cool, then there is thunder, forked lightning, rain. I lie in crisp, white sheets, see Jack digging in a garden, stop, wipe his brow, look up at the sky, and know that memory is a fiction that I can write.

I am sitting on a stone bench in an enclosed garden of pinks, whites, purples, the sun behind a cloud, when a young monk in his thirties strolls near, book in hand. I understand silence, but am not sure that I understand these men.

"Good afternoon," I say, reflexively.

He looks up, nods. "Good afternoon."

I am a bit surprised to hear him speak. "I understand that Trappists take a vow of silence. I'm sorry if I invaded that."

A smile. A shrug. "We minimize unnecessary speech. We are not antisocial. Or mute. You'd be surprised how much speech is unnecessary."

It is my turn to nod. Then: "Would you mind talking to me a bit?"

He lowers his book, studies me.

"Or is that wrong?"

"Not at all."

He approaches, sits at the other end of the stone bench. The sun slides from behind the cloud. I can hear only bees nearby, birds in the distance.

"Is it true that you make wine and cheese?"

He smiles. "Cheese and fruitcake would be more like it. We'll be doing extra work starting in September to prepare for the Christmas volume. It's a source of needed income."

"What else do you do here?"

"There is so much to keep us busy. We have cooks, carpenters, electricians, plumbers, mechanics among us. There are daily tasks: washing dishes, cleaning floors. We run our own waterworks, our own sewage disposal plant. There is a large vegetable garden, a mechanized farm, a small beef herd. We grow and harvest wheat. We have a granary."

He folds his book shut, leans the weight of his body forward slightly, his hands braced on the front edge of the bench beside his thighs.

"I'm Martin Radey," I say.

"Thomas Merton." He offers his hand, which I take. "Where are you from?"

"Toronto, Canada."

"Really? My brother was stationed somewhere near Toronto early in the war. He went to Canada to join the Royal Canadian Air Force. He couldn't wait for us to enter the war."

"Where is he now?"

A hesitation. "He's dead." Another beat. "His plane went down in the North Sea."

"I'm sorry."

"I'm sorry too. It was the mention of Toronto that brought it back." A pause. "How long will you be with us?"

"Three days."

"Like Jonah."

"Pardon?"

"In the belly of the whale."

I smile. "A nice whale, though." I look around me.

"Have you been here before?"

"No. This is my first time."

"Have you been to Kentucky before?"

I shake my head. "No."

"What brings you here?"

"What brings anyone here?" Then, as before, I surprise myself. "I have a son who lives in Kentucky."

He nods, as if understanding. "Near here?"

"Ashland."

"That's in the eastern part of the state. Did he tell you about Gethsemani?"

I think about it. "Yes," I say. "He did." Then I ask him, suddenly, the sun in his face, the memory of lightning flashing in the night, of Jack leaning on his shovel, staring at me, of the trip here, of my years alone: "What is a monk? What is this place?"

He smiles, frowns. "Does the silence scare you?"

I do not know what scares me anymore, can think of no answer.

"Monasticism is rooted in all major religions of the world. It was practiced in the East a thousand years before the Christian era. Gethsemani has been here for a hundred years. A monk," he says, looking away, "is not a man with a fiery vision. A monk has nothing to tell you except that if you dare to enter the solitude of your own heart, you can go beyond death even in this life, and be a witness to life." He turns to me. "You can be a monk, just by accepting that. It is a process, not a destination."

I look at him, into his dark, confident eyes.

He stands, picks up his book. "Pray for me," he says, nods, and leaves.

The sun beats down warmly on my neck, my back, as I lean forward, hands clasped, elbows on my knees.

* * * *

"Tell me about your son."

It is the next day. We are in the garden again, on the same stone bench.

"He runs a hotel in Ashland," I say. "The Scott Hotel." I see Jack in a shirt and tie, hair slicked down, at a large desk in a private office.

Thomas Merton nods, looks down. "How old is he?"

My mouth is dry. "Midthirties," I say. Jack signs a form, folds it, places it on the side of the desk.

"I'm thirty-three," he says.

I look at him. "You could be my son. I could be your father." You could be Jack, I think. He could be anywhere.

"My mother died when I was six. My father died when I was sixteen."

We are quiet.

Then, sitting here, beside him, the past surfaces. I remember another priest, at the graveside of my baby brother Patrick, more than sixty years ago. I remember him telling mother that Patrick had been redeemed.

In this garden, with this man, the question flows naturally, yet surprisingly: "What is redemption? I don't think I understand."

He squints, smiles. "It's an interesting theological concept. Very complex. The root meaning is to set free or to cause to be set free. To redeem is to ransom. The Old Testament saw redemption as a transaction. One could be redeemed by sacrifice, by giving of self. We were capable of our own redemption. The New Testament, ah, now that's slightly different. It is imbued with a redemption for which God paid the price."

I feel the sun warm my hands, listen to the silence around us.

"Men need to be set free from a power greater than themselves, but it cannot be accomplished without cost. Someone must pay. Man or God." He stares out into the rush of summer colors: impatiens, petunias, white roses, baby's breath, soft mauve forget-me-nots, moss rockfoil, dark red.

On the third day, I sit in the same place, hoping, then finally knowing, that he will return, and he does not disappoint me.

"I'll be leaving tomorrow morning," I say.

"I've enjoyed our conversations," he says. "Will you see your son before you head back home?"

My eyes waver, then focus on a rose arbor, arched and bowed, climbing with red and green. "No," I say. Jack opens the door of his Dodge roadster, climbs in, checks the rear-view mirror.

He hears more than I say, tilts his head. "I had a son," he says.

I watch a pollen-heavy bee lean forward into a daisy.

"Both he and his mother were killed in the war, during the firebombing of London. I never married her. I never saw him."

I am quiet for a moment. "You didn't have to tell me."

He is calm. The air is still. "We only seek," he says, "to avoid unnecessary speech here." He turns, looks at me. "Has your trip been worthwhile?"

I look up. A lone hawk is circling high in the blue August Kentucky sky. "It's been good." Then: "It's been inevitable. It's like I've been drawn here."

"I know." He looks at me. "This is the center of America."

I watch his eyes. They focus on a point I cannot see.

"This monastery is holding the country together. This is its heart. I have a hermitage less than a mile from here. I write by candlelight at sunset, view the valley, the woods from my window. One has to be in the same place every day to realize how rich the uniformity is. The solitary life is awesome. It can shock you, and it can give you grace. We discover our eternal dimensions in the midst of our failures."

He reaches down, picks up a stone at our feet, rubs it clean, hands it to me. "Here."

I hold it in my palm.

"This stone is life."

I say nothing.

"It exists before and after death."

I close my hand over it.

"It is all that we have, all that we are, all that we will be."

I squeeze its hard, unyielding surface.

He offers his hand. "We are all monks," he says. His hand waits.

"Thank you," I say.

"Good-bye, Martin."

"Thomas."

"Pray for me," he says.

Before I board the bus to Bardstown, I walk once more among the array of small white crosses on the hilltop, feel the earth giving gently beneath my feet, among silent men who lead silent lives, among my brothers. My fingers touch the small stone in my pocket. And from a corner of my eye, cowled in white, retreating into an arched doorway, I see Jack, my son, fading into the stone walls.

5

MARCH 1949, AT AGE THIRTY-NINE, MARGARET HAS ANOTHER baby, a son, Dennis. Anne, Ron, Judy, Leo, and now Dennis.

On my way back from the hospital, ahead of me on the streetcar, with my eyes still open, in blacks and whites and grays I see Jack brushing a daughter's hair, straightening up the collar of her coat against the cold, then pull the cord above his head. They leave by the side door.

On Saturday, September 17, 1949, the Great Lakes excursion ship *Noronic* catches fire at its pier in Toronto harbor. The single exit blocked, the ship's fire hydrants dry, one hundred and eighteen people die.

I dream that in the smoke, Jack is trapped, looking for me.

A warm, beautiful Saturday, weather in the seventies, just before her twenty-second birthday, October 14, 1950, Joan marries Al McLeod. During the reception at the Old Mill, my sister, Mary Rossiter, four years widowed, in her eighties, drinks too much wine, but no one cares.

Margaret and Tommy are here. Jock is here. Things are good.

And then everyone is waiting. I must dance with her. One dance. It is expected.

There is a spotlight, the circle widens and we are alone. As I move about the floor, my daughter in my arms, I realize that it is the same: I am touching Joan at last, lifting her, like Gramma in the cold room onto her bed so many years ago.

"Thank you," she says, and squeezes my hand. The words, with her face radiant, are a gift, all that I want. Joan is my second chance and I have not failed. There will be no further losses.

I smile back, for me a rare smile, dance foolishly to the music, sway, and when it is over I surprise myself when I kiss her on the forehead, my heart thudding, and see that she is still, gloriously, smiling back at me.

I light a cigar, pull my hat low over my brow, and watch as Joan and Al leave for Niagara Falls, unable to believe my eyes. Then, in the instant between joy and regret, between loss and possibility, I turn and fancy that Jack lights a cigarette beside me, his eyes sparkling.

On Christmas Day, 1950, I board the streetcar, heading to see Margaret, to see what is left of my family.

And then it happens. The blue candle goes out and it is my turn to die.

Coda

The wind owns the fields where I walk and I own nothing and am owned by nothing and I shall never even be forgotten because no one will ever discover me. This is to me a source of immense confidence.

—THOMAS MERTON
The Sign of Jonas

In 1984, in the hospital room, Jack, as unreal as I am, hands Margaret a rose, which seems real, which she clutches in her bent hand. Their bond is stronger than I have ever understood, born of shared experience of which I have not been a part. I have nothing to give her, nothing that can match this, but Margaret does not mind. Her hand would still hold out the nickel, give me everything. She has always asked for so little, and now is no different.

My Margaret. Dying alone, as so many others. I think of my brother, my sisters, of all our children, and wonder how someone with so much family ends up so alone.

Oh Maggie. Margaret is ours. Where are you?

And then suddenly, Jack and Margaret are gone, the hospital is gone, the instant has vanished, and I am once again spiraling upward on black wings, turning, the sky above endlessly blue and white. My destiny as a father is over. My family, I understand, is scattered on the winds.

Higher.

The voice in my head is my mother's, teaching me, pointing to objects, naming them, saying the words. Time happens to the world around me, but not inside, not to memory, because memory is beyond time, traveling forward with me, forging lives out of life, shaping the earth, the sky, the heart.

I am higher than I have ever been before, clearheaded, lungs bursting, can smell the sea, other lands, can see farther, almost to Ireland, a loy digging in green hills so far away, and Elora the bridge over the Grand the Tooth of Time the blacksmith's shop Sarah Patrick Loretta, now the Nipissing the hayloft at Boyd's farm the Queen's Hotel Brookfield Street Constance Street Pacific Avenue a Killarney razor and a shaving mug with a brush made of badger hair a silver thermos Da on the side of the road covered with canvas a Homburg hat a dancing bear a bottle of Lourdes water a smoking stand and a hassock, the Scott Hotel Fire Proof Moderate Price Tub and Shower Baths the rose arbor at Gethsemani

the hawk falls on me from above finally yes talons shredding my feathers piercing my heart where all things are won and lost and I feel Maggie's fingers touch my face Gert's breath in my mouth and then I look into the hawk's eyes fiery blue and see that it is Jack and understand as I hear him sing at last it is so perfect yes understand what I have been waiting for how it was to happen why it was to happen and am grateful

am carried higher into the white clouds small heart pumping ecstasy as I join my family my sisters my brothers on the four winds vision dimming and look one last time at the hawk's beak spreading my breast crimson one last time to see that it too has changed oh changed yes and am filled with joy as I see Gramma open her mouth about to speak to me yes oh yes for the first the very first time.